# Deadly Jewel

SAM TAYLOR

Cover art by Patricia Burn

ISBN: **978-0-9873202-1-6**

# A PLANET FORBIDDEN TO ALL

Zokar Rizian is a cold-blooded murderer and a self-seeking scavenger. But in committing an unexpected act of friendship, he becomes an unlikely hero. Laura St James is just an unsuspecting girl trying, with little luck, to be just like everybody else. She does not consider herself a terrorist. But with one impulsive act, all that changes and she becomes an unlikely villain. These two just can't get it right. Things get a whole lot messier when they are forced into an uneasy alliance to protect a planet that nobody else thinks is worth saving – Earth.

The story begins with a dying soldier's confession of what he saw at Area 51.

# PROLOGUE

The old fellow was ex-military, but he was obviously senile.

'Area 51?' said the croaky voice, from the tiny kitchen. Tom returned with a black coffee which he placed before the reporter, Anthony.

Anthony glanced at the pictures of men in U.S Army uniform on the wall, the edges yellowed with age. He noticed there were no pictures of children or family. The room smelled of musty old books and the faint scent of lemon cleaning agent.

Tom laughed, and seemed more lucid. However, his strange words belied the impression of rationality. 'Yes, yes, there were aliens. God, those grey aliens were like deer on the highway. We were always scraping them up and taking them away before they freaked out the locals. I remember dragging them out of people's houses and out of their backyards. We even had hypnotists on staff to convince those poor people that they had seen bald coyotes, or escaped monkeys.'

He sighed, and leaned his large frame back into the chair, fiddling with a frayed piece of upholstery on the corner of the armrest. Anthony looked at the gnarled hands engulfing the coffee mug.

'No, it wasn't that there were aliens, son. The thing about Area 51 was that when they found that pod, with those aliens… they found a child with them. A human child, or mostly human, by the look of it. They were protecting it. The aliens both died and we were left with this… little blond child with big grey eyes. It was hurt and scared, and too young to talk much. Those alien suckers were wrapped around it, protecting it, like they wanted it to live.'

He lapsed into a long silence, then stirred, his voice going gravelly with emotion, 'And what the hell did we do?'

Anthony leaned forward and waited for more of the story. He

2

was taping the interview, and even if the old man was a complete lunatic, this would make a great fiction story.

'We tried to *dissect* it, well her. We took this little girl, she was frightened, alone. A pretty little thing and we strapped her to a steel table. The medics were going to *dissect* her.'

Tears welled in Tom's eyes and he whispered, 'What are we, that we could do that to her?'

'You 'tried.' You didn't succeed?'

'Succeed? You call that a success?' He glared at Anthony, his brown eyes dangerously hard. Then his anger lost momentum and he looked as though he were lost in memories as he took another swig of the whiskey.

Anthony felt guilty for giving Tom so much alcohol, but not too guilty. It was getting him one hell of a story.

'We couldn't. The other guards and I, we'd seen them do dozens of those aliens, you know, dissect them.' He swallowed, 'Sometimes alive...' he took a large swig of the whisky, sucking desperately on the bottle, before he went on, 'But when the medics put that little girl up on that steel table... I started shaking my head, then one of the other guards, he just said, 'No!' and before I knew it, we all stepped up to the table and said, 'No,' to those damned white-coated vultures!'

Anthony leaned forward, waiting. Eventually he asked 'What happened then?'

Tom shrugged and smiled humourlessly, 'What do you think happened? There were four of us, each over six-foot-four, with machine guns. Those skinny little medics backed right off. The big guy who had spoken up first, he unstrapped the little girl and lifted her down. She held on to him for dear life, clung to his leg and peeked out behind him. Poor little bugger. Shaking like a leaf, she was. And those eyes, those big silvery grey eyes, that was the only part of her that didn't look human. They had darker rims around the irises and they looked into you, like they saw inside you.'

He shook himself and continued running a hand through his white, frizzy hair. 'The big guy seemed to know kids. He told her his name was Michael. He asked what her name was and she pointed at him and said...'

He stopped and put his other hand up to his forehead, but then went on doggedly, 'Ah, it's hard to describe, she repeated his name, but everything she said sounded... really drawn out and strange. She said 'Miiiii-kellle' and pointed at herself and said 'Lorrrrwa.' But anyway, he called her 'Laura'.' He looked up at Anthony and dropped his hands back to the armrests.

'Then I thought, 'what do we do? We can't fight our way off the base'. Then that young Kennedy fellow arrived and he was like, '*Thank God* you didn't let them,' and he and his aides took the little girl. The big guard, the one that was the first to help her, she took his hand and wouldn't let it go. I guess that's why he went with them. He disappeared after that. I think she may have been allowed to stay with him. It turned out he had a young family and I think they relocated them together. I heard they went overseas, but I don't know where. Maybe Australia.'

Tom's voice had faded away and sounded vague again, so Anthony prompted, 'How long ago was this?'

'Oh... years. Hell it must be... fifteen years. I didn't realise it was so long.'

'And then what happened?'

'Well, nothing. That's the funny thing. There was no disciplinary action and there were no transfers. They just kept us there and we stayed at our posts like nothing had happened, but the next time they brought one of those aliens in, I walked.'

'What do you mean?'

'I couldn't do it anymore, I couldn't watch. Those alien suckers... you see, before that I had thought of them as inhuman and a threat to us, but they... when we found them, they were wrapped around her, protecting her. Don't you see? They were *better* than us. We tried to *chop her up*, for God's sake. They died protecting her.'

There were tears in the old man's eyes. Tears for the loss of faith in humankind.

'What did that make me? A monster, worse than the rest of my God-damned race.'

They both remained silent as the tears dried on his brown, papery skin.

Eventually Anthony straightened his shoulders and said, 'You didn't know.'

'So? I didn't know? Is that a reason to be brutal? No, I'm going to Hell for what I did to those poor bastards.' He took another long swig of the whisky, his Adam's apple bobbing as he

4

took gulp after gulp.

'So, what did you do then?'

'I left the military. John Murphy, my commanding officer came and saw me. He asked me about my loyalty to the Service. I told him I couldn't do it any longer. Loyalty shouldn't be given mindlessly. I told him I liked Kennedy, he was such a *kind* young man but I just couldn't be so hard any more. I have no real regrets. I was only a few years off retirement anyway.'

He waved the whiskey bottle at Anthony. 'The one regret I have is that I wasn't the first to say 'no'. Somebody else had to start the ball rolling for me. Maybe if I had spoken up sooner, started the ball rolling, that would have given me some sort of redemption.'

Tom fell silent for a moment, then sighed, 'But I didn't.' Silence fell but Anthony had one last question, 'Why wait? Why talk about this now, when you haven't said anything for fifteen years?'

Tom smiled oddly and replied in a matter-of-fact tone, 'I'm dying, son. If I don't tell this now, it'll never get told. And who's gonna give me grief about it now? What are they gonna do? Lock me up for the few weeks I have left?'

Anthony left the cottage about ten minutes later, and pulled out his phone as he walked towards his grey sedan 'George, you are not going to *believe* what this old guy told me...'

At the end the reporter's run-down, George asked, 'So *where is she now*?'

'The little girl they found? Who knows?'

'What did you say they called her?' George asked.

'Laura.'

# CHAPTER ONE

'Laura!'

'Yeah?' she called from the garden. She stood up amidst the greenery, dusted black soil off her hands and walked towards her father, who was standing on the back porch. She smiled and stood on tiptoes to give him a quick kiss on the cheek, 'Hi, Dad. How was the conference?'

Michael, who had leaned down to allow her to kiss him, straightened back up and grinned wryly, 'Oh, just great. But don't you have a train to catch?'

'Hmmm?'

'Your mother just told me you have a date with Bill.'

'Oh, that's not until seven. I don't have to catch the train until six.'

'Sweetie, it's five o'clock now, you know.'

'Oh, dammit!' she exclaimed, and toed off her dirt-covered boots hastily.

Michael laughed and said, 'Don't panic. Now that I'm home, I can run you down to the station. Oh, and....' he handed her a shopping bag, 'I bought you that blue blouse you admired last week.'

'Oh Daddy, thanks!' she smiled, hugged him and peered into the bag, 'You shouldn't have!'

'Hey, just don't wear jeans with it,' he called as she ran into the house.

He wandered into the house, ducking as he went through the door and called, 'Sandra?'

'In the kitchen.'

He walked into the kitchen and hugged his wife, 'Hey, sweetheart.'

'You gave her the blouse?' Sandra turned soft grey eyes up to him and smiled.

'Sure, I like Bill.'

She laughed, and reached up to tousle his dark, but silvering

6

hair, 'What, you'd send her in a coal sack if you didn't approve of him?'

He changed the subject and took a deep breath in, 'Huh... what's cooking?'

'Roast beef and potatoes.'

'Yum. I'm starved. I haven't eaten anything but hamburgers since I left.'

'Oh, that'd be right, living on hamburgers. Well, if you don't mind, can you stay out of my kitchen? I don't want to get distracted and burn myself,' she said, pulling on oven gloves and heading for the modern gas cooker against the wall.

'I love distracting you,' he said, tugging her back towards him.

She slapped his hand away and said firmly, 'Right, that's it, out! Go set the table.'

He sulked out the door, ducking as he went through it, and said over his shoulder, 'I told Laura I'd run her to the station at about ten to six.'

'Okay, I'll slow the roast down.'

Laura came out of the shower and hastily dried herself. She unhooked her hairdryer from the wall, dried her pale blonde hair, then checked out her cupboard and its neat row of clothes. She picked out a plain dark blue skirt and shimmied into it before pulling the silky deep blue blouse out of the bag on her bed. She tugged the price tag off it then pulled it over her head and smoothed it down. The colour made her silvery eyes stand out, she realised, looking in the mirror.

She tossed the tags, bag and tissue paper in her waste bin, then moved back to the mirror and sat down to put her makeup on. She loved the new Swiss brand of makeup that Trudi had given her for her birthday: the subtle, paler colours blended much better with her fair colouring.

She ran down the stairs at ten to six, tripping in her haste. She fell, but time seemed to slow down and she grabbed the rail. It was only after she righted herself that she realised that her father was standing at the bottom of the stairs, staring at her. By the look on his face, she realised that he had seen what had happened. He sighed and tightened his lips. As she passed him, he grabbed her arm gently.

'Sorry,' she said.

'Don't apologize. Just don't tell anyone, okay?' he said.

'Yeah, yeah, I know.'

'You look absolutely stunning.'

'Thanks,' she mumbled, blushing.

'Come on, you're late. Go say goodbye to your mother and I'll drop you at the station. Got your phone?'

'Yep.'

'Call me, if anything happens, but call me anyway, when it's time to come home.'

'Okay. But Bill's nice, Dad, you know that.'

'I know, sweetie, but boys...'

She laughed, 'If he gives me any trouble, I'll go all bad-ass on him and kick his butt.'

His grin froze. Although he knew to her it was just bravado, he knew what she was capable of.

'Come on, hurry up.'

'Sir, yes sir!' she teased.

'Bye Mum!' she called as she headed cheerfully for the front door.

'Come and give me a hug, you terror! I haven't seen you all day!' said her mother.

Laura groaned, raced back into the kitchen and hugged her mother.

Sandra exclaimed, 'Laura, you still have dirt under your fingernails!'

Laura carefully picked the dirt out from under her nails as her father drove to the station.

They arrived ten minutes later and Michael let her out at the curb, 'Bye, and be careful.'

'Bye, Dad.'

She waited until he was out of sight, then turned to climb the steps of the station just as the train whooshed into the station.

She swore and ran awkwardly in her high heels over the concrete and steel pedestrian overpass, then down the stairs. At the ticket machine she waited for it to print her ticket, then sprinted for the train as the doors began to swish closed. She jumped and made it through the doors just in time.

She felt something slow her down and heard a ripping sound. She turned, to see her beautiful new blouse torn, leaving a gaping hole on the front of her left sleeve.

She almost tripped as the train started moving and grabbed the back of a seat to stay upright. Her face screwed up in anger as she examined the damage to her blouse and she felt her mind send a blast of fury at the train even as it occurred to her that it was illogical to blame a train for anything.

The train slowed, then the interior lights dimmed around her and flickered out. The usual roar and whine of motors and movement went quiet, so all that could be heard was the sound of the puzzled passengers talking. Momentum carried the train a few more metres along the tracks, but not far enough to reach the end of the platform before it drifted to a silent stop. An eerie silence fell.

After a long silence, the intercom over their heads crackled into life and a male voice announced, 'Uh, ladies and gentlemen, there will be a delay of about twenty minutes, er, due to a malfunction in the train's cam batteries.'

'What's a cam battery?' wondered Laura. The woman standing next to her shrugged.

The announcer's voice came back on, 'Ladies and gentlemen, I have now been informed that the delay may be up to forty-five minutes. The train doors cannot be opened automatically without power, but if passengers wish to disembark and find other forms of transport, they are welcome to open the doors manually, as we are still adjacent to the platform.'

A couple of men in Laura's carriage stepped up to the doors and manhandled the levers which opened them. Fresh air flowed into the carriage from outside. Laura hopped out.

She pulled out her mobile phone and dialed, 'Dad, hi, the train broke and I need a lift.'

'The train broke? What? I'll be right there,' Michael said, 'Are you okay? You sound upset.'

'I'll talk to you when you get here.'

Ten minutes later the blue Ford pulled up to the curb where Laura was waiting. A maintenance crew had already arrived at the station. Michael stared at the truck which was carrying a forklift and had a team of men in orange jumpsuits surrounding it. 'What happened?' he asked as Laura sat down in the passenger seat.

He looked at her carefully. Her face was pale, and she looked subdued.

Then he noticed the tear on her blouse and asked, 'How did that happen?'

She looked at the sleeve of her blouse and said, 'It got snagged.'

He turned the car around and stopped at the exit of the car park, waiting to turn right onto the main road.

'How'd it get snagged?' he asked.

'On the train door, when I was hopping in.'

'Okay, I'll take you home and you can change. I can drive you in to town. Don't worry, you won't be late. I'm sure Bill would understand anyway if you were,' he said, reaching over to ruffle her hair.

She nodded, then fell silent.

After a minute his curiosity got the better of him, 'What happened to the train?'

'The batteries all died.'

'But it's electric,' he said.

'Apparently it needs a battery to hold the cam up against the electric line to get at the power.'

'Oh. I didn't know that,' he said.

'Neither did I.'

'So what drained the batteries?'

She shrugged miserably, 'Same thing that happened to everyone's phones, I suppose.'

Michael looked outside the car and saw people hammering uselessly at their phones and joining the long queue to the public phones at the station.

'But sweetie, how did you call me? Is your phone working?'

'Yeah.'

He sat back and frowned, then saw a gap and pulled out into the traffic.

They drove in silence before she turned to him and said, 'Dad?'

'Yes honey?'

'I think I might have done that to the train.'

'What makes you think that, baby?'

'I.... I was angry, because of my blouse being ripped. You just gave it to me, and it just, it upset me.'

He looked thoughtful and replied, 'Jesus, Laura, if you did that, that's quite a bit of power you're talking about there.'

'I was really pissed off.'

He sighed and ruffled her hair again, 'Remind me not to annoy you, darling. But anyway, no-one was hurt, were they?'

'I guess,' she said, fiddling thoughtfully with the ring that Trudi had given her for her last birthday, 'But what if I'd been angry with a person, not just a piece of machinery?'

He didn't know what to say and met her eyes with a worried look before turning his eyes back to the road.

Michael dropped Laura off and she greeted Bill with a cheerful hug saying, 'You wouldn't believe the time I've had getting here.'

He smiled at her, 'Well, you're here now, that's what counts.'

Three weeks later Laura stared incredulously at Bill in the corridor at school, 'Why?' she asked, leaning on her locker with one arm, her books in the other.

He crossed his arms and looked away, 'I've... met someone else.'

A purring voice in Laura's ear whispered, 'Someone who puts out.'

Laura spun abruptly and watched Shauna Williams link her arm to Bill's and stroll provocatively off with him down the corridor. Her school blouse was two sizes too small, her legs tanned and toned with her skirt hemmed up to the maximum limit. Laura buried her head in her locker to hide the hot tears that threatened, 'You bitch.'

Her eyes squinted shut with pain and rage, but somehow she managed to stop the tears from escaping. She slammed the locker shut, spun the dial to lock it and trailed up the corridor.

A crowd of people blocked her way.

'What's going on?' Laura asked and worked her way through the crowd, only to freeze with horror as she saw Shauna on the floor with a trail of blood coming out of her ear. Bill was leaning over her, shaking her.

Someone called, 'Get an ambulance!'

Someone else yelled, 'Get a teacher!'

'She's dead,' whispered the girl next to Laura.

Laura's heart began to thump faster and faster in her chest, then she turned and fled the building and ran towards home. When she got home she let herself in through the back door, ran upstairs and threw herself on her bed. She buried her face in her pillow, and thumped the bed with her fist, trying to get the image of Shauna lying crumpled on the floor out of her head.

Trudi St James, Laura's big sister, arrived home that evening, bouncing in the front door, her silky hair swinging, her soft grey eyes alight. She had her mother's slender, willowy frame and her father's jet black hair. She hung her school bag on the row of hooks in the hallway and followed voices into the kitchen.

She said breathlessly to her mother and father, 'Did Laura tell you? Shauna Williams collapsed at school today. She nearly *died*. She's going to be in intensive care for weeks.'

Michael and Sandra turned to her, horrified. Michael asked, 'What from?'

'They said it was a brain aneurism.'

Michael demanded, 'What were you doing listening in?'

Sandra said distractedly, 'Laura's home already? I didn't hear her come in.'

'Oh, Daddy, it happened right there in the school corridor. It was awful, but it was... cool.'

'Trudi, that's awful!' her mother said.

'But, Mum, if I'm going to be a police officer I'll have to learn to deal with this stuff, you know that. I won't be like Bill, sobbing and going to pieces.'

'Bill?' Michael asked.

'Yeah. He's her boyfriend. That guy that took Laura out a few weeks ago.'

Michael was starting to look very worried.

Sandra looked puzzled, 'He's her boyfriend? But I thought he was still Laura's boyfriend.'

'No, they must have split, because he was with Shauna. Everyone's known it for the last week.'

Cold chills were beginning to travel down Michael's spine, and he grabbed Trudi's arm, 'Did *Laura* know it?'

'Well, yeah, I guess. Well, I don't know,' she flinched 'ow, you're hurting me.'

'Where's Laura?' Michael asked, already on his way upstairs, taking them two at a time.

Michael found Laura on her bed, sitting with her knees drawn up to her chest, eyes shut, rocking back and forth. He walked over to sit beside her and hugged her, and she burst into tears, 'Oh Daddy, Daddy, I killed her.'

'No you didn't, sweetheart. Trudi just came home from school. Shauna's in intensive care but she's going to live.'

Eventually she looked up at him, hiccupping and white-faced, and said, 'Daddy, take me away. Take me away from people, please.  Somewhere far away.'

He sighed and nodded, stroking her hair, 'I think that might be a very good idea, possum.'

# CHAPTER TWO

The dark blue Ford swung around another bend, heading uphill, as it had been for the last twenty minutes. Laura and Trudi were singing together in the back seat of the car.

Michael laughed and said, 'You two know you can't sing to save yourselves, don't you?'

'We don't care, Daddy,' Trudi laughed, 'What now?'

'How about 'Row Your Boat'?' Sandra suggested.

'Yeah, you don't need to be able to sing to do that one,' Michael grinned, and reached for the bag of chocolate drops on the dashboard. They slid away from his fingers and he made another grab for them, but they slid out of reach. He glanced into the mirror and saw Laura looking cheekily at him. He raised an eyebrow at her and the girls started singing another tuneless song.

The Ford rolled on up the road, packed to bursting with suitcases. Ahead of them, a truck with 'Global Removals' printed in big letters on the side contained their furniture. Michael watched amazed as the truck swung around another corner and looked as though it were going to teeter over and fall down into the lush greenery which covered the mountainside.

'I can't believe they're letting you work from home,' Sandra said happily, over the noise of the girls' singing.

'Oh, everything's different these days, love, you know that,' Michael smiled, but he looked thoughtfully in the rear view mirror at the girls, 'They get on well, don't they?'

'That'll never change,' Sandra said.

'I hope not,' Michael said, chewing his upper lip, and Sandra looked fondly across at him. He shifted, annoyed that his hair was touching the top of the car's cabin.

They arrived at the farm about twenty minutes later. Michael turned up the long gravel drive towards the neat white stone building. When the car came to a stop the girls jumped out and ran into the house, while the truck pulled up beside the house and the removalists started unloading furniture.

Later that morning, as they unpacked, Trudi set up her computer in her room.

'Thanks Tru,' Laura said from behind her.

Trudi looked up at her bedroom door, 'What for, Lor?'

'I know it's going to be harder for you, doing it by correspondence.'

'Nah, I'll be fine. I spent half my time in school bored anyway. This way I'll be able to study for two hours a day instead of six. You're doing me a favour, Lor.'

Laura walked over and hugged her 'But thanks, anyway.'

Trudi hugged her in return, then went back to fiddling with the computer, 'You'll miss me when I go away next year.'

'Yeah. I'll survive.'

'Girls!' Their father's roar came from outside, they looked at each other bewildered before running outside.

'Daddy!' Trudi shrieked with delight while Laura stood horrified.

Two brand new trail bikes stood in the front yard, and their father was paying the man who had delivered them.

The man turned and said, 'Wow.'

Michael looked at him and followed his gaze to the two girls.

He stepped up to the man and looked down at him, 'Off you go, buddy.' Michael glared after the truck as it drove away.

Trudi was on her bike, and a deafening roar destroyed the tranquility. She spun her bike experimentally in a doughnut around her father, 'I love you Daddy!' she screamed happily at her father and took off down the driveway, a shower of gravel marking her confident progress.

'Wait, Trudi, your helmet!' Michael roared, but Trudi didn't hear him.

Laura wordlessly took the helmet he offered her and bounced up and down on the bike a few times, then shrieked as the machine burst into life.

She took off after her big sister, the bike surging awkwardly as she figured out the gears and snaking across the grassy areas on the drive. She clung on fiercely as she followed Trudi's lead down the driveway.

Trudi roared back up the long driveway and past Laura, her dark hair streaming back from her face as she screamed, 'I think I'm going to love living in the country!'

Up at the house, Sandra came out into the garden and said wryly to Michael, 'You could have waited until they unpacked.'

He shrugged and grinned, putting his arm around her waist, 'Yeah, probably. But hey, this isn't such a bad idea after all, is it, love?'

She smiled and shook her head.

Later that evening, Trudi walked out into the yard, 'Lor?'

'Over here.'

Laura was sitting down, head tipped upwards, looking at the sparkling river of stars that seemed so close it looked like they were about to fall down into her lap.

'What are you doing out here?' Trudi asked.

'Relaxing. Can you hear that?'

'What?'

'Exactly. It's... silent, Trudi. I think this is the first time I've ever heard silence.'

'It is quiet, isn't it?'

'Yes, and that horrible jabbering has gone.'

There was a silence, then Trudi asked curiously, 'What jabbering, Lor?'

'You know... what people think.'

Trudi shook her head, but Laura didn't see her in the dark.

'God, it's amazing. It's a side-on view of the galaxy,' Laura said. 'A planet with a view.'

'You're funny,' Trudi chuckled, 'Who thinks like that? Who says that sort of thing?'

'Doesn't everyone?'

'No.'

'Do you ever wonder if there's anyone out there, Tru?'

'Nope.'

'Do you ever look up and feel like you should be screaming out for someone to come and get you?'

'Definitely nope.'

'You have no soul, Trudi.'

'I'm human. I have a soul.'

Laura looked at her askance and said softly, 'Other people have souls, you know.'

'What?'

'Not just humans.'

Trudi sighed, 'Come on, sis, it's time you went to sleep. We've both had a big day.'

Laura sighed and stood up, following Trudi back into the house. Laura went into her half packed room and was asleep within moments.

The dream started with the view of the starscape, a bright wash of glowing stars, strangely unblinking. Then her perception drew back from the image and she realised that she was in a small spaceship. She was strapped into a seat, too terrified to speak.

Amidst the inky blackness ahead, the deep blue circle that had been rapidly growing before her, had transformed itself into the ground below her. The trouble was that ground was a long way below her, and she was falling towards it too fast. She felt the sudden gripping terror of falling from a great height and whimpered.

Laura thrashed about on her bed in her sleep and cried out.

Michael and Trudi came running into her room. Trudi stopped and wondered when her sister had time to unpack and put away all her possessions. Michael didn't notice, but sat down on the bed and shook Laura gently by the shoulders.

'Hey, snap out of it baby,' he said.

Laura's eyes snapped open and Michael jumped and Trudi yelped as all the boxes and bags that had been lying around in Laura's room suddenly crashed to the ground around them.

The next morning, Laura and Michael both sat subdued at the breakfast table. Laura's mother, oblivious to the events of the night before, looked out the window, enthralled by the tiny finches that darted about in the bush outside

Sandra smiled and said to Laura, 'Come and have a look at these birds, darling.'

Laura stood up and walked over to look out the window, 'They're beautiful. So cute.'

'They have eyes like yours,' Sandra said.

Laura blinked and took another look at the birds.

'But they're really silver, Mum.'

'Yes, exactly darling.'

'Hmph,' grumbled Laura and sat back down.

'Morning, I just unpacked all our jewellery.' Trudi fastened Laura's gold chain around her sister's neck.

'Oh, thanks.' Laura reached up and touched the cool metal.

Laura went outside after breakfast and Michael looked at Trudi,

'Why did you put that gold necklace on her, Trudi?'

Trudi looked at him, 'Haven't you noticed, Dad? She always calms down when she's got it on.'

# CHAPTER THREE

The five Galactic Union Battle Cruisers turned sharply and began the slow run through the next few light-years of the Perseus arm of the Milky Way.

The great ships had a utilitarian look about them, were planned with long rows of airlocks, escape pods and banks of sensors. The ominous round snouts of various calibres of weaponry provisioned the vessels at every available junction. No vessel could approach a Galactic Union Battle Cruiser from any direction without finding itself facing an impressive arsenal of weaponry.

Within each vessel twelve hundred men, women and elves slept, worked, or engaged in some sort of recreational pursuit.

In the command chair of the largest of the vessels sat Domhan Keallach, a tall young man with jet black hair, dark eyes and a powerful build. He sat staring at the moving starscape, occasionally checking the work of the scanning crews.

His communications officer said, 'Incoming message for you, Lord.'

'Viewer,' he glanced at his second in command behind him, noticed that the man was standing stiffly at attention, and guessed where the message was from. Domhan flicked a finger at the view screen in front of them, then sighed, suppressing the look of dull resignation that came across his face. 'Hi, Mum.'

Arlene Keallach was a small, jet-haired woman, dressed in a soft, indigo robe, the luxurious material in sharp contrast to her fine, austere bone structure. She looked at him with a sweet smile, 'Come home, darling.'

'You know the answer to that.'

'Please. I don't want to grow old and die without seeing either of you.'

'That's a laugh. Anyway, you'll see both of us, as soon as I find her.'

She stared at the stubborn young man on the view screen in front of her, 'Four years old, you were, when you took your first ship out, Dom. Do you really think you are ever going to find her?'

'It's a big galaxy. Might take a while.'

A shadow of sadness crossed her face as she shook her head, 'They tell me you are out in the Perseus arm?'

'Yes, Mum.'

'Be careful. It's pretty wild out there.'

'I've been out in the galaxy for twenty-two years. I can look after myself.'

'I know dear. You need to get a life.'

'I will, when I find my sister and return,' he replied absently running his fingers over the scanner controls on his console and taking a quick look at the readouts.

'Alright sweetie. Bye for now. Love you.'

He flushed slightly, 'Yes, Mum.'

The communications officer was terrified she was going to crack a smile, and that Domhan Keallach would kill her for laughing at him. Her fears were well founded; he had shot his first yeoman when he was ten. He had a hell of a temper back then. He had mellowed with the years.

Domhan stood up and paced around the bridge several times, then said to his second officer, 'Take over. I'll be in my quarters.'

He strode through the ship, finally reaching his sumptuous main quarters in the centre of the ship. He had austere battle quarters up near the bridge, but rarely had reason or inclination to use them. He heard the doors close behind him with a quiet swoosh, then wandered over to his bed and lay down with a sigh. He rolled onto his back, then turned his head to the view screen which showed the steadily moving stars.

He sighed, and rubbed his forehead and said aloud, 'What the hell am I doing?'

He got up and collected a coffee, then stood before the view screen sipping the hot drink and silently watching the dull starscape drift by.

After many minutes he whispered, 'I know you're out there somewhere. I can still feel you.'

He tossed the cup into a square hole in the wall. There was a soft red flash as the cup disintegrated and he strode out of his cabin again and began to prowl around the ship. Crew members scurried out of his way, hastening to appear busy. Domhan ignored them and strode on, knowing that his mere presence on a regular basis would keep the crew alert and the ship running smoothly.

# CHAPTER FOUR

Back on Earth, life went on as usual. Trudi had been away for many years now, first at the Police Academy, then at her first post in Sydney. The welcome news that Trudi had been posted closer to home, in Brisbane, had cheered Laura up immensely. Her sister could now visit on weekends and often did so.

Laura had started training young racehorses for a local breeder and liked to ride out the back of the farm along the forestry roads which were soft and sandy and went for miles through endless rows of huge pine trees.

Today however, Laura was bored. Her parents had left on a cruise two days earlier, their first holiday for many years, and would be gone for three more weeks. It was dull at the farm without them or Trudi. Laura had volunteered to mind the animals for them and was regretting her decision to stay at home. She was glad Trudi was visiting this weekend. Laura finished her chores and decided to take one of the young horses out for a ride. She was supposed to wait for Trudi to ride with her, but Laura figured she could exercise one horse before Trudi arrived, then only have two more to exercise after. They could take those two out together, then come back in plenty of time to catch a movie at the local cinema.

Thirty minutes later, Laura was having trouble with the difficult young mare she had chosen to ride. The big black thoroughbred had been broken in and in training for three weeks, so it should have stopped playing up. However, either the damned animal was obstreperous by nature or it was plain stupid. She found a large boulder beside the path and used it as a mounting block to remount the fretting animal… or would have, if the beast had not jumped away as soon as she tried to put her leg over the saddle.

She fell to the ground with a thump and swore again. 'Great, twice in two minutes, going for a record are we?'

At her next attempt, by virtue of the monkey strap and some fast legwork she managed to mount the horse, which nonetheless was cantering off with her by the time she had both legs in the stirrups.

'Bloody stupid thoroughbred nitwit,' she grumbled mildly.

She knew it was no use taking her annoyance out on the horse, so she just let it settle into a rhythm along the path and prayed that no more man-eating bunny rabbits jumped out at them.

She rubbed the bruise on her leg and asked the horse, 'How many rabbits are in the stream-bed next to your paddock? *Hundreds*. And how often do you shy at them? *Never*. But one bloody baby bunny jumps out in your way out here and you dump me in the dust!' She spat grit out of her mouth and decided to take the longer route up to the TV tower. Maybe a good long hard ride would sort the frisky big black filly out.

Laura relaxed a little, feeling the warm sunshine on her arms and shoulders and enjoying the rhythmic movement of the horse galloping beneath her. Her mobile phone rang and she fumbled to reach it, but the horse beneath her heard the strange noise, stopped abruptly, spun around and bucked hard. The ground came up beneath Laura with a hard bang and she was sitting on her very sore butt watching the black's rear end race up the path, disappearing into the distance towards home.

'Shit, shit, shit - ouch!' she swore.

A distant voice from the ground a metre away alerted her to two facts, firstly she had managed to answer her phone before being dumped and secondly she had dropped her phone.

She ferreted it out of the grass beside the path and snapped, 'Yeah?'

'Do you always swear like that at people?' Trudi asked.

'Oh, hi Trudi, sorry. I just got dumped.'

'Oh, jeez, are you alright?'

'Yep, fine, just got a long walk home, that's all,' Laura said.

'Need a lift? I'm driving over anyway.'

'Oh, okay Tru, could you pick me up... ah, at the coffee shop on the main highway just past the strawberry farm? I'll be there in five minutes or so.'

'Yep, no worries, I'll be about ten minutes. I'll meet you at the café and we can grab coffee.'

'Okay, thanks.' Laura limped across the paddocks towards the café, hoping she wouldn't bump into anyone she knew, so she wouldn't have to explain why she was at the café without a car or a horse. At least the horse had galloped off along the forestry road, which went back to their farm without crossing any roads with traffic.

Laura ducked through the tight strands of a barbed wire fence with practiced ease, shimmying between the lines of wire so that no part of her body touched them, and trudged on. The sun was getting hotter and she took off her helmet, swinging it casually beside her, her blonde hair, which had been dark with perspiration, drying out to its usual silvery sheen. She ducked through the last fence and walked towards the café.

As luck would have it, her friend Sheree was on shift and she quickly assessed Laura's dusty jodhpurs and grazed hand and said, 'Coffee's on the house, love. Need a ride home?'

Laura pursed her lips ruefully, 'No, I'm fine, thanks, just the coffee. Trudi's coming to pick me up,' and she waved her mobile at her, 'I managed to hang onto this.'

Sheree chuckled and brought her coffee quickly, but before they could resume their conversation Laura heard the sound of galloping hoof beats. *That's more than one horse.* She ducked outside and froze. There, galloping along the main road on a silvery white horse, was a slight blonde woman. She had the reins of the big black horse in one hand, leading it. She was looking intently towards the ground, then slowed down and walked the horses in to the parking area outside the café.

'Is she *tracking* me?' Laura wondered out loud.

The small blonde stranger looked down at Laura, assessed the dusty jodhpurs and riding boots and wordlessly handed her the reins of the black horse with a nod.

Laura stared at her. There was something strange about her. She was slight and blonde, with a narrow triangular face and strange big eyes. They were grey, but looked more silver than grey, Laura decided. The eyes looked odd. She realised they had wide dark rings outlining the silver irises, which made the strange colour stand out even more. In the sunlight, her hair had an iridescent sheen, making it look almost silver. Her skin was fair, but lightly tanned. Then Laura remembered her manners and stammered, 'Th-thank you!'

The blonde girl jumped as though from an electric shock when Laura spoke. The white horse jumped too, perhaps feeling the jolt of its rider's muscles against its sides and mistaking it for a signal to move. The rider held the single rein tight until the horse settled down. Laura was busy checking her black mare over for injuries. There didn't seem to be any. Finally, Laura looked back up at the blonde girl's horse and realised that it was not wearing a saddle. The bridle was just a thin strap over one ear of the horse, holding a noseband, a single rein and no bit. There was something very odd about the pair of them, the girl and her horse.

The girl was staring at Laura like she had seen a ghost. She asked, slowly and carefully, with an accent Laura could not place, 'Did you just say, 'thank you'?'

Laura smiled up at her, 'Yes, thank you, for my horse. For bringing her back to me.'

The girl's head tilted more and more to the side as Laura spoke, and she seemed fascinated, 'You understand me! You speak? How do you do these things?'

Laura pursed her lips and squinted up at her, raising one eyebrow at the odd questions and said, 'Same way you do,' Backpackers! Foreign chicks were always weird.

'You understand me,' the girl repeated, fascinated by that single fact.

'Well, you might have a foreign accent, but your English is pretty good.'

Again there came the slight nod. The girl looked around, suddenly looking a little anxious and asked, 'I had thought to find you injured, but you are not? Do you wish me to wait while you remount?' Her voice was quiet. She seemed almost terrified.

'I have to wait for my sister. I called her and she's driving up here to meet me.'

The stranger frowned, then nodded and stilled. Her horse stood quietly.

*Her horse is not breathing hard*, Laura realised. Laura's horse, the black, was standing with sweaty sides heaving, trying to get its breath back after the gallop. The nearest access from the forestry to the main road was three miles away, so they must have covered at least that distance because they had come back via the road. Yet the slight foreigner's horse was standing there as though it had not done anything. The horse was silky white, with blue eyes. 'Your horse, he's beautiful. I've never seen such a silvery white colouring.'

The foreign girl stroked the horse's mane with soft fingers, and looked puzzled, "Horse'?' She pronounced the word slowly as though she had never heard it before. Then she looked at Laura with those intent eyes and asked, 'My shimmel?'

'Is that his name, Shimmel?'

She stared at Laura and shook her head, as if not understanding what she meant. Then she inspected Laura closely and said, 'You are not quite Fey. But you are, a little.'

Laura screwed up her face, puzzled, 'Who's Fay?' and thought to herself, the chick might be on drugs, or just really dumb, or just having a lot more trouble with English than I thought.

The stranger shook her head in frustration and said, 'We speak the same language, yet we do not quite understand each other. You are not of the Fey.'

Laura was completely lost by now, so she responded, 'Probably not?' Had the girl said Fay, or Fahey? Did she mean her surname was Fahey? Laura waited, but the girl was not forthcoming with any further comments. Laura shuffled her feet on the hot gravel, checked the black horse's girth and bridle and considered mounting up. Perhaps the girl would talk to her if she was up at her level. She might be a weird foreign chick on drugs, but she hadn't done anything hostile and she had brought the black mare back.

The girl seemed to come to a decision and stroked her horse with one long stroke along the neck. The horse kneeled briefly, allowing her to dismount gracefully and stand next to Laura. She smiled up at Laura, 'You are tall. From up there, I thought you were very short.'

'How did you teach him to do that?'

'What?'

'Kneel down when you dismounted?'

'Oh, that. I taught him when I was a child and too little to mount.'

'But how?' At the back of Laura's mind the thought came unbidden, and how have you owned him since you were a child, if you are foreign? There were strict quarantine laws making the importation of horses into Australia prohibitively expensive.

'It is easy. I will show you.' The strange girl stepped up to the black mare and stroked her the same way along the neck. To Laura's amazement, the black horse shuddered, then knelt down.

'What the hell? But how did you?'

'They will all do it, you simply have to let them know,' She looked guilty, as though she had said something she shouldn't have. She said, 'Your sister, is that her?'

Trudi was turning into the driveway in her white Ford. Laura nodded. How did she know that was Trudi? Probably a good guess.

Trudi drove up and asked through her open window, in a horrified voice, 'What's wrong with your horse?'

'Oh, nothing, Trudi, I was just going to mount up,' Laura took the opportunity to impress her sister and mounted the black, which then lurched to its feet and stood staring at the blonde girl.

'Trudi, this is… I'm sorry, what did you say your name was? Fay?'

'I did not,' said the blonde girl, smiling and then tilted her head, as though listening to something in the distance, 'I must go,' she said, 'People are worrying about me. Goodbye.'

The white horse bowed briefly and she leapt lightly onto its back, her legs wrapping around the horse's ribs and tucking in behind its elbows. She gave Laura another close inspection as if memorising her face, then turned and galloped away, disappearing into the early twilight. The black tossed its head, but did not try to follow.

'Who was that masked woman?' Trudi asked.

'Well, that's the funny thing, she didn't really say. She brought my horse back, but she wouldn't tell me much. Bit of an oddball anyway, if you ask me.'

'Pretty. Foreign, probably a backpacker?'

'Hmmph.'

'Did you notice that she had six fingers on each hand?' Trudi asked.

'Bullshit.'

'Yeah-ahhh. Oh yes, she di-id,' Trudi grinned at Laura.

'You're making that up.'

'I don't make things up,' Trudi said.

Laura had to admit that her sister was not the imaginative type. She was a policewoman, not given to flights of fancy. She stared after the girl.

'Did you find out anything about her?'

'Her horse's name is Shimmel and I think her surname is Fahey.'

'Well, that's something.'

# CHAPTER FIVE

Over the next few weeks the black filly got more work than Laura usually put into a freshly broken in horse, partly because it needed it and partly, if she was honest, because she was hoping to bump into the Fahey girl again. She had no luck, and when she tried to look up Fahey in the local directory, found nothing. It had occurred to Laura, however, that a foreign backpacker wouldn't be in the local phone book.

The funny thing was Laura had been riding through the forestry for years on her own and felt proprietal about the area. At first she had wished for someone that could keep up with her when she rode, but after a while she just enjoyed the solitude and the ability to go as fast as she wanted. It wasn't until she saw the easy way the blonde girl sat her horse and realised that she was probably a better rider than Laura, that she started to feel bored again riding by herself. Laura started to ride faster and further on each ride, attempting to alleviate the boredom by galloping and cantering more. It wasn't working.

She rode through the forestry exploring more thoroughly than she ever had, venturing up unknown paths, up onto the rocky crags where wallaby droppings and the shuffling noises of lizards were the only signs of life, and travelling along stream beds that were well off the beaten trails.

The black horse heard it first, ears pricking up with interest, so she followed the direction of the horse and then she heard it, the sound of rushing water. Laura rode closer and came across a series of rapids, which she followed upstream to their source; a small waterfall five metres high. There was a deep pool at the foot of the falls and the white horse Shimmel was grazing quietly on the lush grass between the boulders beside the pool. Laura froze and scanned for signs of life. Eventually she spotted the foreign girl, sound asleep on a large round boulder with a smooth, flattish top. She was stark naked and her sleek body shimmered in the sunlight.

God, these European chicks are so unselfconscious. Damn, she thought, what do I do now? If she went up to the girl and gave her a fright, she had the feeling that she would never see her again. But if she didn't, she may not find her again either.

The problem was solved for her as the white horse looked up and whinnied loudly and the black responded. The girl sat up and looked at her, then casually stood up and gathered her clothes from where they were draped to dry over a bush, put them on and walked over towards Laura. Laura had politely turned away. The foreign girl spoke from behind her.

'Hello again.'

'Hi,' Laura turned around.

'You are far from your usual territory.'

'Yes I, actually I was looking for you.'

'Why?' the girl's voice was polite, curious.

'Oh, I don't know, it gets kind of boring riding out here by myself and you seem to spend a bit of time out here. I thought maybe we could ride together occasionally.'

The foreign girl looked at her with those big silver and grey eyes, and asked, 'Do you not have' then stopped, and looked flustered, 'other people to ride with?'

'None that can ride like you,' Laura smiled, then held out a hand, 'My name's Laura St James.' She was wondering what the girl had been going to say before she stopped herself.

The foreign chick looked completely perplexed and stared at her hand, then jumped as Laura reached over, took her hand and shook it a few times before releasing it.

The girl rubbed her hand, looking puzzled. Laura suddenly wondered what country she was from. She hadn't been able to place the accent up until now, even though she was usually quite good at picking accents.

'So, what's your name?'

'They call me M'Rel.'

'That's nice. Who are 'they'?'

'The others.'

'You ride with friends?' Laura was hopeful, a group of riders who could ride like M'Rel? Now that would be fun.

'Yes, but I do not know whether they could talk to you, because I could not understand your sister.'

Laura stared at her, puzzled. What did she mean, she didn't understand Trudi? The foreign girl had been speaking fluent

English to Laura since they met. What did that have to do with whether her friends would talk to Laura? Laura started wondering if she was going daft.

'Huh?'

'I shouldn't be near you,' M'Rel said, looking frightened.

'Wait, don't go,' Laura said, as M'Rel turned to leave.

'I must. We are not supposed to associate with the locals,' said M'Rel as she headed towards the white horse. M'Rel was definitely foreign then.

Laura turned to mount her own horse straight away rather than walking after M'Rel. If M'Rel was going to ride off, Laura had already decided to follow her. She knew she'd never catch M'Rel if the girl got a head-start on horseback.

Laura's instincts were spot-on. M'Rel leapt onto the silver-white horse and was gone. Laura kicked the black and followed immediately.

Laura should have known better than to try to keep up with Shimmel. They wove in and out of the trees, jumping logs and winding their way through rough territory. The black stumbled and Laura lost her seat as the horse fell, her head connecting hard with a log.

When she woke up she was in a cave with a soft, dry moss floor. Someone was arguing. It was M'Rel and a man, who had the same silver eyes and blonde hair. A relative? She tried to listen, but they were talking a foreign language. Laura faded back into unconsciousness again.

Laura awoke later to find that she was sitting before M'Rel on Shimmel. They were both on the white horse and M'Rel was using one arm to hold Laura before her and steer the white horse. With the other arm, held out to the side, M'Rel was leading the black horse once again.

'Hey,' Laura muttered groggily, 'How long was I out?'

'Two days,' M'Rel answered.

They came up to a roadside, where there were several four wheel drives and other vehicles that looked like police cars, until Laura saw 'Search and Rescue' on their sides. About twenty people were milling about. M'Rel rode towards the group. Arms reached up for Laura as she started fading into unconsciousness again.

Then she heard shouts and galloping hoof beats and a male voice beside her saying ruefully, 'Well, she's gone. We'll never find her in there.'

Laura spent a week in hospital, then was back out at the farm convalescing, driving Trudi up the wall. She was a lousy patient and she was dying of curiosity about M'Rel.

After another week she saddled up the black again. Trudi looked silently at her, then saddled up a big bay thoroughbred and said, 'I'm coming with you.' Her frustration with her little sister's addiction to danger had long ago been worn down to worried resignation.

Laura shrugged, 'I'll be fine.'

'Not if past performances are anything to go by, and besides,' Trudi admitted, 'I'm curious too.'

'Okay.'

They got to the front gate, though, and M'Rel was riding in on the white horse, looking extremely nervous.

Laura stopped her horse.

Trudi stared at M'Rel riding up to them. It struck Trudi that the girl looked more than foreign. In the bright sunlight of mid-morning M'Rel's hair shimmered more than the silver horse she rode and her eyes were very bright with a strange sparkle. If Trudi didn't know better, she would have sworn that M'Rel's skin was a little more translucent than it should be, too.

'Laura, she's not,' Trudi stopped as Laura rode up to join M'Rel. She had been going to say, 'She's not human,' but stopped herself, because it dawned on her why M'Rel's appearance had been bugging her from the day they first met. Trudi realised seeing Laura and M'Rel at the same time, that they had the same colouring: the same silver-blonde hair and pale grey eyes with dark rims around the irises. Trudi said nothing, but the thought was still very much in the forefront of her mind.

M'Rel smiled when she saw Laura. 'You are alright. I was worried about you,' Trudi was surprised because the girl spoke a foreign language, but she smiled politely and said, 'Hi, I'm Trudi, Laura's sister. We almost met a couple of weeks ago.'

M'Rel looked wide eyed at Trudi and turned to Laura, 'I am sorry, I cannot understand her. What did she say?'

Laura lifted a hand, gestured at M'Rel, then at Trudi, then looked back at M'Rel and said, 'W-what?' If there was one thing she couldn't abide, it was people being rude to her sister.

M'Rel flinched under the sudden irritation in Laura's eyes and said softly, 'Laura, please, I don't… I must go.'

Laura sat on her horse dumbfounded as M'Rel turned and galloped out the gate. Trudi rode up next to her and stared after the girl and said, 'What the hell was that about? And what language was she speaking, anyway?'

'English,' Laura replied abruptly, wondering if both the other girls had gone mad.

'No, it wasn't,' Trudi said, 'anyway, why did you talk to her like that? You've upset her.'

'She speaks English, Trudi. That was English.'

'No… it… wasn't.'

The sisters glared at each other, both sure of what they had heard.

Laura looked at her sister and started to wonder. Trudi was not a liar and she wouldn't joke about this. If Trudi said M'Rel was speaking a foreign language, she wouldn't have made it up. Laura had thought M'Rel had been rude to her sister, but now Trudi was saying she didn't understand M'Rel? It dawned on Laura that a misunderstanding was occurring and she didn't want M'Rel galloping out of their lives without getting to know them because of a misunderstanding.

'I'm going after her,' she said and kicked her horse into a gallop.

'The hell you're going without me, little sister,' Trudi muttered and galloped after her.

Trudi caught up to them a kilometre up the road. The blonde girl was talking that strange foreign language to Laura and Laura was speaking back, in English. They both turned to Trudi as she rode up and the girl asked her a question in the strange language.

'What?' Trudi asked.

Laura fell suddenly silent and stared at them. Trudi looked at her and said, 'Laura, if you don't know what language that is, how come you understand every word she says?'

'It's English, Trudi. I understand it because… it's… English!' Laura's voice was beyond exasperated.

'I've said it before and I'll say it again. No, it's not English.'

'I think I need therapy,' Laura groaned. It was not enough that M'Rel was the weirdest foreign chick she had ever met, but now her ultra-sane sister was having a meltdown.

Trudi sat in thoughtful silence for a moment as her detective training kicked in and she tried a more logical approach than yelling at her sister, 'So, when she speaks in that language, it sounds like gibberish to me, but English to you? And when I speak in English, she can't understand me, but when you speak in English, she can understand you?'

'What did she just say?' M'Rel asked Laura.

'Oh, I am stuffed if I know, M'Rel. Even I didn't understand that little rave,' Laura answered.

Trudi turned the bay horse so that she could look at them both, 'The thing is, Laura, she doesn't speak English. Doesn't speak it, or understand it. Unless it's to you.'

'What the hell does that mean?' Laura demanded.

'Good question,' M'Rel added quietly, wondering what Trudi had just said.

'It means that you're the only one she can understand,' Trudi suggested.

'Well, how does that work?' Laura asked.

'I don't know. What I do know,' Trudi said, 'Is that we have one very strange creature here, and I don't think she's from around here. Not from anywhere you or I know of, anyway.'

'So what, she's foreign? Well, duh.'

Trudi got snappish at the sarcasm in her little sister's voice, 'Duh, indeed. Hey, she has six fingers and reads your mind. I think that's a little more than 'foreign', don't you?'

Laura fell silent and looked at Trudi. She glanced at M'Rel, then back to Trudi.

'Reads my mind?' Laura asked.

'Well, how else do you want to explain that she understands what you are saying?' Trudi said.

'Well, why can't she understand you, then? Can't she read your mind?' Laura said.

'I guess maybe not? Why don't you ask her?' Trudi suggested.

Laura raised an eyebrow. Sometimes her sister made a great deal of sense. She turned the black filly around to look at M'Rel.

'M'Rel, can you read my mind?' Laura asked.

M'Rel squinted at her, and said, 'Not very well. You are not Fey. I can read you enough that when you form words, I can understand your words. However, I cannot understand hers.'

'Not very well.' Laura stared at her, slowly taking in her response. Not 'no', not 'can I do what?', but a simple 'not very well.'

'So you can read my mind?' Laura asked.

'Of course. How else could I talk to you?' M'Rel said.

Trudi's eyes were wide. She had heard Laura's side of the conversation, 'So she can read your mind?'

Laura nodded her head and stared at her sister, 'Apparently, but not yours.'

M'Rel turned to Trudi and shrugged apologetically.

'Now do you think she's from around here?' Trudi said.

'Um, not really, but where is she from?' Laura wondered.

M'Rel heard her and raised one arm over her head and pointed straight up in the sky. Laura and Trudi followed her gesture, then stared at M'Rel

Laura looked at M'Rel with awe in her eyes, 'Holy shit!'

Trudi put both hands up to her mouth, 'Oh my God,'

Laura exhaled and looked up at the sky again, then back at M'Rel, 'The Fey? The Fey are from up there?'

M'Rel nodded. Laura looked at M'Rel. Trudi, ever pragmatic, said, 'Laura, ask her if her people drink coffee.'

# CHAPTER SIX

The ship on which Zokar Rizian was second in command, the Reingold, was a huge vessel, one of only twenty of this size that the Galactic Trade Alliance, ran amongst its fleet of thousands. It was two thousand metres long, and had a crew of over a hundred and fifty. It was jet black, but had the red and gold logo of the Galactic Trade Alliance displayed on sixteen sides. It was a giant of a ship, like a giant cylinder but with eight long slab sides and a nose cone at each end. It had a large cargo bay built to accommodate the occasional major salvage operation. The cargo bay could take a Galactic Union Battle Cruiser in its entirety, and had done so on several occasions. Mostly, the Reingold transported mining and agricultural bulk products between the planetary systems of the outer Galactic Union. Its captain, Shiva Kiran, and his second in command, Zokar Rizian, were always on the lookout for more lucrative cargo and often took jobs on an opportunistic basis, such as small salvages and interplanetary prisoners and hostages.

The Galactic Trade Alliance served the Galactic Union well, but being a commercial operation, the Galactic Trade Alliance was always coy about how much their ships moved and earned. There were two things inevitable in life, death and taxes. The Galactic Union was fond of doling out both, one for disobedience, the other for financial gain. In light of this fact, the Reingold had more than one computer system: one official, and another which only the captain and second in command ever accessed.

The central bridge of the Reingold, where Zokar sat, was a large octagonal room, about twenty metres across and five metres high, deep in the interior of the vessel where it was well protected from enemy fire. It gave the impression of being out in open space because every wall overhead and the ceiling were covered with view screens which showed the view from different sensors around the ship. The effect was that of sitting in open space, with windows all around them. The crew of the Reingold was very efficient. Zokar had often wondered why it took twelve hundred soldiers to crew a

Union Battle Cruiser, when the much bigger Reingold got by with a hundred and fifty. Perhaps, it was because the crew of the Reingold all shared in the profits their vessel made, and were more motivated than the Union soldiers.

Zokar sighed. He was sitting in one of the two dozen seats fixed around the walls of the room, facing a daunting array of sensors, screens and readouts. He glanced at his scanners again, then cocked his head. Was that a hyperdrive trail? It was faint and obviously old, but it was definitely there. He leaned forward and ran expert fingers over the board before him, examining the characteristics of the trail. He plotted its trajectory, then looked at the scanners and ordered a course change towards the star system in its path. It was only a couple of parsecs off their path. He knew that hyperdrive trails with this signature often signified a ship that had been in trouble and that was a potential salvage opportunity.

Elesk noticed his sudden interest, 'Something, sir?'

What they found was far more valuable than salvage. Living like demi-gods amidst a primitive tribe on the fourth planet of the system, they found two Gentrakians. Not far from where they were living was their wrecked ship. They had crash-landed there many years ago. Gentrakians were large, dark green, semi-reptilian, many-tentacled workers. They were physically tough, which is why they had survived, but they were not engineers. They didn't have the technical expertise to repair the ship or to bring their ship's computers back on line.

Zokar found some very interesting records in those computers. He took them to his captain, Shiva Kiran, in his quarters. Zokar did not want this knowledge known to the rest of the crew. He personally maintained the security in his and Shiva Kiran's quarters, so he knew that both cabins and the computers were secure.

Shiva Kiran was in his early twenties. Often his compatriots and opponents thought this would make him an easy mark, but they were soon disenfranchised of that concept, along with their cargo and wealth, if they were not careful. The soft blonde hair, the youthful, tanned face, the slave-boy good looks of the purebred human: they were misleading. On closer inspection some people detected the diamond-hard glint in the blue eyes and the lightning-fast mind behind the sweet smile.

That lightning-fast mind was something he had in common with his elvish first officer, Zokar Rizian. Elves did not give their loyalty easily and when they did it was only to those they considered their superiors. Anyone who gave it any thought quickly realised that a creature like Zokar would not be scavenging around the galaxy with someone who was not his equal.

They made more than a decent living for themselves and their crew as part of the Galactic Trade Alliance. Their ship was well-equipped and well maintained and their crew highly disciplined and more loyal than one could expect from a mixed crew of humans, elves and the occasional part-Fey. Shiva and Zokar were more willing than most Traders to dare the outer reaches of the galaxy, which meant that the Reingold's work was more risky and more lucrative.

Zokar had the exotic, slanted features and delicately pointed ears typical of the old-elvish. He was tall, young for an elf and powerfully built with silvery white hair, darkly tanned skin and silver eyes. Many people were taken aback by the platinum orbs, which gave him a cold, calculating appearance. An accurate assessment if you did not know him, but Shiva Kiran knew the fires that burnt beneath those cold eyes and treated his second in command with deep respect, bordering on wariness. They had formed an unlikely friendship, unspoken of course, but it had lasted for several years and the two had learned that they could rely on each other.

Shiva leaned over and stared into the viewer, on which two common Grey aliens carrying a small bundle ducked into a powered escape-pod and the airlock doors closed behind them. There was a sudden flash of blue light, and the escape pod disappeared. Zokar leaned in close watching the viewer.

Shiva turned to him, surprised to find his second officer so close and asked, 'Do you think you can calculate the trajectory of this escape pod? The main ship was moving at the time, it might be difficult.'

Zokar gave one of his rare smiles and handed Shiva a data-ball. 'Already computed and encoded, sir.'

'Where did they go?'

'Earth.'

'You have got to be kidding me. With the infant?' Shiva's voice was incredulous as he leaned back in his chair.

'Apparently. I surmise that they considered it would be the last place anyone would look for them. Also it is the only place where they could both hide and control the infant,' Zokar said.

'Hmmm, I see your point. But what do you consider the chances of the infant surviving on Earth, even if they made it there?' Shiva asked, rolling the data ball thoughtfully in his fingers.

'Normally I would say slim. However considering the nature of the infant, perhaps it survived,' the elf said.

Shiva looked at Zokar, 'That infant would be an adult by now and probably a formidable one.'

'Formidable yes, but not impossible to control. Earth has the suppression field. It should be possible to subdue the creature whilst still within the field, then sedate it to keep it unconscious,' Zokar said.

'But with the suppression field operating on Earth, how would we find the creature in the first place?' his captain asked.

The elf pursed his lips and said, 'We have scanner records from the original missing persons file from the Galactic Union. The old hand-held scanners are adequate, they can scan DNA mixtures within a few hundred metres and they operate on older technology which won't be affected by the suppression field. It may take several weeks and it will take a great deal of manpower, but it can be done.'

'Really,' Shiva tossed the data-ball up and down in his hands, 'the DNA records are on here, too?'

'Yes, of course.'

'I wonder if the Alliance would allow us to travel to Earth to look for the heir? If we found the child'

'Adult,' Zokar corrected.

'Yes, adult… the rewards would be,' Shiva leaned forward.

'More than we could make in a hundred years running ore and salvages, Shiva.'

Shiva Kiran turned and looked into his elvish second officer's silver eyes. Zokar Rizian looked as thrilled as he was.

'I'll check with Head Office, but they'll let us go. We're the only ship in this region,' the captain said.

'In the meantime, what should I do with the Gentrakians? If they remember enough, they could lead others to Earth.'

'I doubt that they knew originally, or remember enough to do so. Twenty-two years is a long time. They wouldn't have been able to analyse the escape pod's trajectory without access to their computer records and without that knowledge they wouldn't know where to start looking. They no longer have the records anyway. We do. Is their ship fully stripped?'

'Yes, the teams have worked quickly,' Zokar said.

Shiva said, 'Incinerate it. As for the Gentrakians, memory erase them for the last two days, and release them back to their primitive friends. No doubt the events of our arrival will provide a much-needed boost to their credibility with the villagers.'

Zokar nodded. Shiva was so... kind. It was a quality Zokar admired in his leader, but found difficult to understand. Elves weren't a kind race. They sought out weaknesses and when they found those weaknesses they exploited them mercilessly in order to destroy their opponents. Zokar worried the Gentrakians were a loose end, albeit one which could do them little harm.

Shiva sensed his mood and put a reassuring hand on his shoulder, 'Looks like we're going to Earth, my friend.'

Zokar frowned and admitted to himself that he found the idea intriguing, 'Earth, the forbidden planet.'

'Yes. The forbidden planet. I've always had in the back of my mind that it would be interesting to go there.'

Zokar sighed, 'You would.'

He stood and excused himself politely and left his captain's quarters. Once he was sure he was out of earshot of Shiva, he stopped at a communications unit on the wall. He glanced back towards his captain's quarters and hit the communications unit button.

'Brig?' Zokar said.

The brig supervisor answered, 'Yes sir?'

'The two Gentrakian prisoners we just picked up,'

'Yes, sir?'

'Vaporize them.'

'Aye, aye, sir.'

'Oh, and make it look like an escape attempt.'

'Understood, sir.'

# CHAPTER SEVEN

Trudi poured the third coffee and put it on a tray with the other two. She carried it into the lounge room, her socks whisper-quiet across the polished wooden floor. M'Rel was perched on the pastel sofa like a cat about to jump out a window. Laura and she were conversing animatedly, but Trudi could only understand Laura's side of the conversation. Trudi sat down on the chair and listened.

'When was that?'

The response was a rush of foreign gibberish, or rather, alien gibberish, Trudi corrected herself.

'But how have you survived?'

More gibberish ensued, then a shrug, and M'Rel gazed out the large windows at the trees beyond.

'You've said 'we' a couple of times. How many of you are there?' Laura asked.

That seemed to hit the girl, Trudi noticed. Her shoulders slumped, and she came out with a single alien syllable, followed after some hesitation with more words, spoken in a quiet, sad voice.

'Oh no, I'm sorry,' Laura reached out and patted M'Rel's hand which seemed to puzzle the alien.

'What's she saying?' Trudi asked quietly.

'Oh sorry, I keep forgetting. They crashed here five years ago. There were twenty of them, but only ten survived the crash and only four are left now.' Laura picked up a coffee and nodded gratefully to Trudi.

M'Rel's face looked pinched as she listened to Laura. She reached hesitantly for the coffee cup that Trudi offered her, but flinched back from the heat in the cup. Trudi put the cup down on the coffee table.

'What happened to the other six?'

'She didn't say. Trudi, I really think we should leave this particular topic until later.'

Trudi nodded, then asked, 'Okay, ask her where their spaceship is?'

'Where's your ship?' Laura asked.

This resulted in a flood of alien gibberish and an expressive wave of one of M'Rel's arms towards the forestry and a sad shake of the head.

'She says it's hidden in the forestry, but they can't get it working.'

M'Rel watched as Laura translated for Trudi, then she spoke again. 'What?' Trudi asked.

'She says that until now they haven't been able to talk to anyone. And if you look weird and can't talk the local language, it's best to hide. But if you're hiding, you can't get parts.'

Trudi watched as M'Rel hesitantly imitated Laura in picking up and nibbling at a biscuit from the coffee table, then took a larger bite from the biscuit.

'So they could repair it?' Trudi asked, but then something struck her as odd. 'Laura, if they're smart enough to build a spaceship, and they've had five years, why haven't they been able to learn the language?'

'Good point. M'Rel,' Laura asked, 'If your people are smart enough to build a spaceship, how come you haven't tried to learn our language?'

M'Rel tilted her head and said something in alien gibberish that made Laura smile. Then the girl said something else that made Laura frown with concentration.

'Well?' Trudi was sitting on the edge of her chair.

'You're so damned impatient, Trudi!' Laura said, 'Well, she said she only flies spaceships, she doesn't build them. But they've all tried to learn the language. They cannot understand the syntax, it's too different.'

'We got a bunch of dumb aliens on our hands?'

'Trudi!'

M'Rel asked something and Laura answered her, 'Nothing. She was being silly,' but she shot Trudi a warning glare.

M'Rel took another biscuit, but looked warily at the hot coffee cup and left it alone.

Trudi asked, 'So they can only understand you, because it's like, direct mind-to-mind communication and the syntax doesn't get in the way?'

'I'm guessing that's right.'

'So does she know why you can mind-read aliens? I must have missed alien mind-reading 101 in high school,' Trudi chuckled.

Another conversation took place.

'She doesn't understand that either,' Laura said, adding some more milk to M'Rel's coffee. She handed the now lukewarm cup of coffee to M'Rel who took a cautious sip then screwed up her face in disgust and put the cup back down.

Trudi looked at Laura, 'Pity. But hey, since they can talk to you, is there any chance we can help them? Any chance we can take a look at this spaceship and see what parts they need?'

Laura took in a deep breath and said, 'You're just a stickybeak, Tru.'

'Well, duh, who wouldn't be, about this? Besides, it's my job to investigate things,' Trudi said.

'I'll ask her. I don't know if they will trust me enough to show me their ship,' Laura said and M'Rel started shaking her head

'Trust us, you mean. I'm coming too. I don't want you riding off into the forestry to meet a bunch of aliens, without a bodyguard,' Trudi said.

It took a lot of persuading for Laura to convince M'Rel that Laura owed her one and wanted to help. Eventually the sisters prevailed and they left the house together, saddled the horses back up and set out. They rode for about two hours, cantering a lot of the way. Laura and M'Rel seemed fine, but Trudi was starting to feel the physical strain of riding for so long by the time M'Rel held up her hand to stop them. M'Rel called out something in the alien gibberish. 'Don't move a muscle,' Laura murmured to her sister.

With a jolt Trudi realised that three more of the silver-haired people like M'Rel had seemingly materialised out of nowhere around them. They didn't look happy, but the one nearest to Laura, a lithe, silvery eyed man, had swung his head around to look directly at Laura when she spoke. He asked, 'What did you just say?'

'I was warning my sister not to move,' Laura replied, 'I don't want her hurt.'

'You speak strangely, yet I can understand you. And you look Fey. Please explain,' the man's voice was wary.

'Apparently I can communicate with you people for some reason. I wish to help you.'

'Why?' he asked.

'If I help you get your ship going, will you take me out there with you?' Laura asked.

The Fey man demanded of Laura, his eyes hostile, 'Again, why?'

'Your friend M'Rel saved my life. I wish to repay her. Also I wish to go into space, to see what's out there,' Laura replied.

Trudi interrupted, 'Are you mad?' she turned her horse and moved it up to Laura's, 'Do you know what you're asking? You don't know these people, they could take you up and shove you out an airlock before you get past the moon.'

Laura stared at her sister, 'You are kidding me, right? You'd pass up an opportunity like this?'

'Like what? Climbing into a dodgy spaceship with a bunch of alien strangers?'

'You are such a stick in the mud, Trudi.'

The Fey man looked puzzled, because he could only understand Laura's side of the conversation.

He turned to M'Rel and asked, 'Why did you bring this one back to us?'

'Kinshah, she can speak to us and we to her. She is offering to help us obtain parts for our vessel. We could escape this hellhole.'

'Hey!' Laura protested, turning on M'Rel, 'Earth's not a hellhole!'

The Fey all turned to stare at her and shook their heads. Trudi glared at M'Rel.

'Then what is it?' Kinshah asked.

'It's a beautiful place. I don't know what you people are used to. Maybe your planet is nicer, but please, this is our home,' Laura said.

'Amazing,' Kinshah breathed. He stepped closer to Laura and hissed at her, 'We landed here with ten still alive, did she tell you that? There are slitherers here, black long creatures with red bellies. Their venom curdled the blood of three of my people before we realised what they were. My people died screaming and sobbing. There are predators which look like inoffensive grubbing mammals, but they have six inch tusks and they tore two of my men to pieces and ate them! There are tiny creatures in the air which suck on our blood and poison it. Need I go on? And you call this place home?'

Laura said, 'Yes, I do. I'm sorry for what happened to your people, but this is not their home planet. Bad things happen when you are out of your natural environment.'

'You do not understand. No other planet is a hell-hole like this,' he glared at her made a disgusted noise in his throat and turned away, but M'Rel called out to him.

'What do you say, Kinshah?' M'Rel asked.

'How do we know we can trust her?' Kinshah said, 'She may be as poisonous as the rest of the beings on this rock. I should have shot her last week when you brought her here.'

Laura and Trudi exchanged glances, Trudi's enquiring and Laura's murderous. By unspoken agreement they said nothing and Laura did not jump off her horse and choke Kinshah.

M'Rel looked thoughtful, 'She has done me no harm so far. We don't know, but what is our alternative course of action? Inaction? To stay here, like this, until we all die?'

Kinshah looked sober and thought for a few moments, then nodded sulkily, 'Very well. Stranger, what is your name?'

'I am Laura St James, and this is my sister, Trudi St James. She doesn't speak your language,' Laura added

'Nobody does, apparently, except you,' Kinshah observed. He walked over to peer into Laura's face. He stared closely at her for what seemed to be a very long time, then seemed to make up his mind, 'Tell me, can you bring me some platinum?'

'Well, yes, but it would cost a lot of money,' Laura said doubtfully. Once the Fey made a decision, they didn't muck around.

'Do you have a sample of this money?'

'Um, yes, I have a twenty on me,' Laura pulled out a twenty dollar note.

'This is money?' Kinshah asked, 'What is it made of? It looks organic. If we have access to the base elements, the food synthesizers on board the ship should be able to reproduce it.'

'Well, it's made of pulped trees.'

'These things?' He waved an arm around him at the forest.

'Yes.'

'Well, this should be easy to fabricate. We have cut and stored the substance of these… trees, as we have discovered it can be burnt for warmth. How much do you need?' Kinshah asked. Laura looked askance at Trudi who was looking very curious.

'Why are you giving him money?' Trudi said.

'I'm just showing him an example, so he knows what we need,'

Laura said. To Kinshah she said, 'A bagful would be a useful start.'

Trudi raised her eyebrows at both of them.

'Wait here,' Kinshah said, and disappeared off into the bushes. A few minutes later he returned with a beautifully crafted leather saddle bag and handed it to Laura. It was stuffed full of twenty dollar notes.

'How much?' Laura asked.

'How much? Oh, the platinum. About this much,' Kinshah said, holding his hands out before him as though he were grasping a block the size of a house brick.

'So about five or six kilograms,' Laura nodded, 'Well, that might take a while to get hold of.'

M'Rel said to Kinshah, 'What about the transmission points that we need to replace on the ship?'

He sighed and replied, 'We do not know whether their technology even extends to that sort of equipment.'

Laura asked, 'What sort of equipment?'

'Pulse devices, controlled EMF circuits, that sort of thing,' Kinshah said.

Laura looked thoughtful, 'We could take M'Rel to a technology store and see if they have anything that you could use.'

'That would work Kinshah,' M'Rel said, 'She could communicate for me and I could tell her if anything was useful.' The young alien had dismounted from Shimmel and was hopping with excitement.

'But it would involve going into one of their townships. That is not the same as riding around the forestry,' Kinshah looked worried, 'And what if somebody notices your appearance?'

'Sunnies and a beanie,' Laura suggested.

After agreeing to bring back the platinum and some town clothes for M'Rel, the two sisters rode away.

Trudi pointed at the saddle bag Kinshah had given Laura. 'You'd better be careful. I bet the serial numbers on that are identical,'

'We'll just have to change it somewhere.'

'Where?'

'We'll drive into the city tomorrow and change it bit by bit at the shops,' Laura said.

'That'll take hours,' Trudi grumbled.

'Well, it's better than trying the banks.  What if they notice the serial numbers?  You could get in big trouble with your work,' Laura asked.

Trudi sighed, 'Yeah, good point.  The shops it is.'

# CHAPTER EIGHT

Two months after they had found the Gentrakians, Shiva Kiran and Zokar Rizian found themselves heading into the Buffer Zone and towards Earth. The Buffer Zone was a no-go zone which the Galactic Union had established around Earth, to prevent ships from straying within range of the suppression generator and losing power.

Deep in the bowels of their ship the polarizer which would prevent their ship's hyperdrive engines from being compromised began to hum into life as the scanners detected the drop in power in their engines. It was an impressive device, towering over the heads of security guards and the technicians. It was brand new and it would still look new in a thousand years, because its outer shell was constructed from pure gold. It had been purchased on the black market, at a price which cost Shiva Kiran the best part of his takings for a year, but he considered it well worth it. Considering its origins suspect, Zokar Rizian had gone over it before certifying it fit for use. Shiva therefore had every confidence that it would work now and continue to do so for the next thousand years.

Shiva stared at the view screen. Deadly. Beautiful. Why were so many things that were beautiful, dangerous? Was because the brightest, the most intense colours, were the colours of warning?
A simple blend of blue and green and brown and white didn't sound too spectacular, but as with all things of great beauty... the sum of the parts became more when it became a whole. And when approached from the galaxy's centre, set against the deep blackness of empty space beyond the outer rim, the planet was like an opalescent jewel set in black velvet. Earth. Terra. Sol Gamma Alpha. Erin. It didn't matter what you called it, the names all struck terror into the hearts and souls of most. Earth, deadly jewel of the Outer Rim.

Shiva could not deny the thrill he felt and he was amazed that not once, in all his research, had any of the records mentioned how stunningly beautiful it was.

Shiva paced around the bridge restlessly, then returned to his central chair when the leather on his warrior robes began to chafe his skin. His ship was under silent running conditions and they were not authorised to be here. At least not by the Galactic Union. Zokar Rizian walked up and stood behind him, his face was solemn as he tapped a finger on the arm of Shiva's chair. A miniature video embedded in the chair's arm was displaying details of the landing parties and their preparations.

Shiva glanced down at the six fingers on Zokar's hand. When Elves counted their fingers, they counted the ten of humans, then one elven, and two elven. Yet because each finger was slightly finer than a human finger, Zokar's hands were more slender and graceful than those of the humans around him.

Zokar flicked a button and studied the changing readouts from the miniature video screen, 'Sir, the polarisation device has activated and is performing to specifications. We have full power. The drop in power was only brief and marginal. Also, shields are fully operational. We are invisible to all but the most advanced sensing devices.'

'Very good. Take us into close orbit around Earth then, please Zokar, but monitor our power levels carefully. The teams have been briefed and issued with scanners?'

'Yes sir. Teams are standing by. They have been equipped with Earth-style dress and accessories. Their scanning devices have been disguised as contemporary communication devices.'

'Excellent.'

Zokar Rizian was a good second in command, but he also deserved promotion and his own ship, but at this point in time, Shiva did not have an adequate replacement for Zokar. Perhaps after this mission he might try visiting Zokar's home world and try to hire a replacement, freeing Zokar to pilot his own ship. Shiva would welcome a second ship for his group and if this mission succeeded he would be able to afford one. He couldn't think of a better person to command it.

Shiva's mind came back to their present mission. The Galactic Trade Alliance had decided the chance of finding and trading the young heiress back to the Galactic Union was worth the risk and expense of secretly sending one of their best ships through the buffer zone into Terran space. If this mission was successful, Shiva and Zokar and their crew would be very, very wealthy. Of course if things went wrong, Shiva was under no illusions, the Galactic Trade Alliance would sell himself, Zokar and their crew out in a heartbeat, rather than cross the mighty Union. He knew that they were on their own out on the Rim.

Zokar Rizian stood for another moment beside his captain, then stepped back to his own station to concentrate on the scanners and monitors at his bridge station, because even though they were invisible to all but the most sophisticated of scanning systems, such systems did exist. Notably they were possessed by predator species and by the Galactic Union ships. Zokar had to keep a good lookout, so that he could divert them around such vessels at great distance.

Shiva left his central console and stepped over to Zokar to get a better look at the opalescent planet called Earth.

'Now I know why they call it 'Deadly Jewel,' Shiva murmured.

Shiva stayed beside Zokar Rizian for a few more minutes, watching the more detailed readouts on Zokar's bank of viewers, then paced restlessly back to his central console as the incredible planet grew steadily larger in the view screen.

They were now in orbit around Earth. Shiva looked over at Zokar and noticed that his second in command seemed mesmerised by something on his computer console. It was a welcome excuse for Shiva to leave his chair and walk back over to Zokar's console.

'What have you found?' Shiva asked quietly, peering over Zokar's shoulder.

'Intelligence, sir. An inordinate amount of intelligence.'

'Do you mean native intelligence in the humans, or military intelligence?' Shiva asked.

'Not military. Well, military in the sense that you asked, but not just military. This is amazing, it covers every aspect of their lives.'

'What does?' Shiva asked, growing exasperated. He sat down in the empty chair next to Zokar's.

Zokar turned in his chair, faced Shiva and said, 'They have a computer network, the likes of which I have never seen before. It covers everything, absolutely everything. The sum total of human knowledge, all,' Zokar waved both hands out in an expressive gesture, 'on a computer system.'

'How did you hack into that?'

'I didn't.'

'What?' Shiva asked his face puzzled. He leaned forward to look more closely at Zokar's screens.

'It's just sitting there, for anyone to use. You just have to link to their satellite feeds and there it is.'

Shiva stared at him, hardly comprehending what Zokar was saying, 'You're telling me they have this... hive mind computer network? For everyone to see?'

'Yes.'

'What?'

'Yes, I was quite taken aback too,' Zokar replied.

'But why?' Shiva wondered.

'I do not know,' Zokar said just as puzzled, 'but it seems to be free and its use is unrestricted.'

'What about enemy aliens accessing it?'

'You mean like us?' Zokar smiled.

'Well, we're not enemies. More prospectors or maybe a rescue mission.'

'They seem entirely unconcerned about the possibility of this information being used against them. The thing is, Shiva, with the suppression field in place,' Zokar looked back at his screen, 'they may not think there are any enemy aliens.'

'What?' Shiva leaned forward and held the back of Zokar's chair in one hand.

'They may not think we exist. They would have seen no ships, they are not aware of their own psychic abilities. In fact, from what I can gather from here' he indicated the computer screen with a flick of his silver eyes, 'They may believe that they are alone in the galaxy.'

Shiva stared at the inscrutable silver eyes of his second in command for a few moments, then started chuckling. When Zokar did make one of his rare jokes, it was usually a good one. 'Come on Zokar, pull the other leg.'

'I am serious.'

Shiva stopped chuckling, then tilted his head down and stared thoughtfully at Zokar, 'But surely they realize? Their population geometric progression alone should inform them that they are not a native species. And the differences between humans and other Terran life forms? Not to mention the sheer improbability of such a preposterous hypothesis? These Terran humans aren't stupid

Zokar, are they?'

'No, but they are incredibly isolated,' Zokar replied, 'There simply aren't many stars or planets nearby. The nearest star system is over four light years away. Also their communications and transport abilities are severely hampered by the suppression generator.'

'Give me a look,' Shiva asked and leaned in again to check out Zokar's computer screen. After a moment he said, 'Huh, 'Google'. What a funny name. Type in 'aliens' and see what comes up.'

Zokar complied and Shiva exclaimed, 'Look! There are Greys down there! And shit, are those bugs?   Damn it Zokar, make sure our planet side teams have stasis weapons, if they come across bugs they'll need them.'

'Yes, sir.' Bugs were one of the main predators of human beings. A nice juicy well-wrapped human is practically a necessity for raising each bug larva. The older bugs never seemed to lose their liking of human flesh either.

'Well, this computer system has come in useful already. Probably saved a few of our men's hides.' Shiva shook his head, 'But why? Why do they have such a thing?'

Zokar nibbled on his bottom lip, looking thoughtful and Shiva asked, 'Do you have an idea?'

'A thought,' Zokar replied and spun around in his chair to face Shiva. 'If the Terran humans maintained their telepathic abilities, they would have had some sort of race, species-wide link, no?'

'You mean like the collective soul of the Vintaren? Yes, but Zokar, the Terran humans,' Shiva shook his head, 'They were the most violent humans in the galaxy. Surely they would not have been able to maintain a group mentality? Would they not have turned their mental capacities upon each other and destroyed each other's minds?'

'Not necessarily. Perhaps the suppression generator also saved them from such an eventual fate. Remember, the suppression generator was put in place only after the humans on Earth became a collective threat to other species.   Perhaps, the humans were simply not powerful enough to destroy each other. But consider this, if they were originally a telepathic race, what would happen when that was taken from them with the suppression generator?'

Shiva looked at him, comprehension dawning, 'They wouldn't be able to sense each other's thoughts.'

'Babel.'

'What?' Shiva asked.

'When I was investigating their culture earlier, they have a legend about it. They could all talk to each other, understand each other, and then the Tower of Babel was built, and they couldn't understand each other any more. They attributed this event to punishment from their God.'

'You mean, they knew about the suppression generator?' There was doubt in Shiva's voice.

'Evidently, at the time, they were aware that there was a structure being built and that it had something to do with their sudden inability to communicate effectively with each other. Whether or not they knew where it was, its full effect, or even who built it, is doubtful.'

"God' could have been the Emperor, who would have seemed like a God to these people.'

'Yes, but back to their computer network. *Nature abhors a vacuum*,' Zokar commented and watched Shiva's face.

Comprehension dawned, 'They replaced it! Damn! They replaced their collective soul, with a computer-generated artificial one?'

'Exactly. As soon as they had the technology to do it. It even has translation amongst hundreds of different languages.'

'Amazing, that's amazing.' Shiva stared up at the bank of monitors above Zokar's head.

'Mmm.'

'What?'

'They haven't lost the instincts, Shiva,' Zokar looked at him, 'That makes them as deadly as ever.'

'Oh, shit. You mean, if the suppression generator goes…'

'Yes,' Zokar said, 'They may well form a group mentality. If that happens, they will all have access to it and they will be very powerful. You don't have to look far through their literature so see their longing for some sort of connection. It is still very strong and if they are given their freedom, their minds will be drawn together and will in all likelihood form a most powerful structure.'

'With free access for all. Just like their computer network,' Shiva murmured.

'Yes. And each individual human would have access to the psychic power generated by that collective mind, whenever needed,' Zokar said.

Zokar looked worried, noticed Shiva. Zokar Rizian didn't often look worried, and that worried Shiva.

Zokar continued, 'Shiva, these are *not just humans*. These are the *most violent* humans in the galaxy and their descendants. Have a look at this.'

Zokar pressed another button and Shiva leaned forward and said incredulously, 'These are their crime statistics? murder... rape... what's 'home invasion?' What's... oh my God.' Shiva's voice was quiet, so that the rest of the bridge crew did not hear him. He looked sickened, as he read through the rest of the list that Zokar had brought up. Shiva shook his head as he looked at Zokar, then he gasped as he read the bottom of the list, 'These are yearly statistics?'

Zokar shook his head.

'Monthly?' another shake of the silver head, 'surely not weekly?'

'Daily. In one city.'

Shiva's horrified blue eyes locked with Zokar's silver ones and they both fell silent.


Shiva was suiting up to go planet side when Zokar walked into the ready room.

'Sir, you are not going down there, surely?' The elf was fairly bristling.

Shiva said, 'What, you think the only chance I'll ever have to go planet side on Earth and I'd let every non-com patrolman go down for a look-see and not go down myself? Come on, Zokar.' He pulled the gravnet out of his backpack and checked it before stuffing it back in his backpack. He then checked all the fasteners on his suit.

'If that is your reasoning, then I request permission to visit Earth with you. Sir.' Zokar reached over and checked the suit's oxygen and life support system readouts.

'Denied,' Shiva shot him a puzzled look over his shoulder as Zokar checked the fastenings on his backpack.

'Why?' Zokar was indignant.

'Without me here to run the ship we'll need someone with their wits about them to keep the ship safe in orbit. We're still under threat of detection.' Shiva shrugged the backpack into place, then flinched as strong elven hands reefed the straps tighter. Zokar stepped back around in front of him and glared at Shiva.

'So because you want to go, I can't?' Zokar demanded.

'You can go down later, Zokar.'

Zokar stepped back and pouted, which made Shiva laugh. Elves were such dignified creatures, but occasionally that dignity would lapse and Zokar was no exception.

He was behaving like a small child who had been denied an outing, 'Zokar, you can't come with me every time I go planet side.'

'What I find most disturbing, sir, is that you consider this ship to only have two competent senior officers capable of minding the bridge while the other is planet side. Does that not seem an inadequate number to you?'

'Go mind the bridge. I'll be back before you know it and you can go sightseeing.'

'Aye, sir. Did you check the charge level on that gravnet?'

Shiva tilted his head at Zokar and gave him an exasperated look, 'What am I, a non-com? Of course I did.'

Zokar spun on his heel and left for the bridge. Shiva smiled. He was looking forward to seeing Earth and he could understand Zokar's impatience.

He hooked his gravnet onto his belt, checked all the fittings on his gear once more and headed for the airlock. Once there he passed through the glass doors with twenty other suited soldiers, found himself a marker point on the floor and stood waiting. He and the other soldiers were spread out across the airlock's floor in a circle so that there was no risk of bumping each other when the airlock opened.

On the bridge Zokar gave the order, 'Prepare for airlock depressurisation.'

The giant glass door between the airlock and the ship whooshed shut, and a klaxon sounded. Shiva tested his air once again, and hit a button on the collar to indicate that he was suited up and had air. All the other soldiers in the airlock were also clear, because the blue light came on and the floor beneath them slid aside and they were left hovering with planet Earth far below their feet. The outer airlock door had slid aside, but the ship's antigravity field was still operating, holding them in place. Shiva loved this moment and the adrenalin hit which it caused as his mind reacted on an instinctive level to the absence of the floor and the incomprehensible fall below his feet.

'Stand by for jump.'

The klaxon note changed, the antigravity let them go, and they were falling towards the blue planet below.

# CHAPTER NINE

Shiva wandered around the streets of the strange Earth town. He had assigned his own search grid and he knew exactly how long it would take to cover it. He had also given himself two hours of free time to look around. Rank did have its privileges.

He watched the humans around him with growing interest and delight. These people shouted and seemed fond of an incredible variety of loud music. They laughed uproariously when it suited them, they smiled, frowned, ran, climbed and acted like children. They were so free. They dressed as they pleased with little concern for rank, age or wealth.

He was frightened at first when a huge furry quadruped started to make loud growling noises at him, but a Terran male called to it and it obeyed, sulking back to the human and leaving Shiva with an impression of wild eyes, wild teeth and a rumbling growl. Shiva was shocked. They had wild animals, predators, walking freely among them and the animals did as they bid. He heard a loud regular clatter and a group of children rode across the street behind him, sitting atop monstrous quadrupeds about five times bigger than the one which had accosted Shiva earlier. There were two women with them, laughing and sitting easily on the largest of the quadrupeds, which had long necks and long legs. The animals looked and sounded as though they weighed about ten times as much as any human.

One of the huge animals took fright at the same furry quadruped that had frightened Shiva and the animal plunged about, stood on its hind legs, striking at the smaller creature which darted in and out and growled loudly.

Shiva drew his laser, anticipating trouble, but the Terran male yelled out and the smaller furry animal returned to him. The Terran called out to the young woman, who replied casually and laughed as she sat on the huge animal. About a half a tonne of animal plunged, tossed and pranced under her, hooves scraping on the paved road and she sat on its back and laughed as she chatted to the young Terran male. Shiva stared, entranced. So these are Terran women. This is where Zokar and I will come when we want to find wives, he smiled at the thought.

He noticed the chaotic nature of the traffic and was puzzled, until someone pulled up close to him in a vehicle and he realised that each vehicle was under the control of the individual person sitting in the front. There was a vertical wheel which they used to steer it. It was a horrendously dangerous way to travel, yet the Terran humans did it casually.

When Shiva witnessed an accident, which was inevitable given the apparent lack of sensors or central control of the vehicles, the two Terran males involved left their vehicles and began striking each other and yelling. He was horrified and moved on.

It was a prison planet, yet these humans were free of the tight binds of millennium-old customs that restricted the behaviour of many peoples in the 'free' systems that he had visited. They were wild, free and exciting and they seemed to have formed an incredible, easy bond with many of the other life forms on this beautiful planet. Shiva had never felt so at home as he did wandering around on the wild streets of Earth that afternoon. He walked around a corner and there was a sudden crack and his world went dark.

A small group of teenagers gathered around his still form and started rifling through his pockets, pushing and pulling on his prone body and clothing. Shiva did not stir.

'Man, this guy's weird,' the taller youth said.

'He doesn't have money. Not even a credit card,' grumbled his companion, a slight teen boy with braces.

'C'mon, let's go.'

'What about this stuff?'

The taller boy shrugged, 'Might as well bring it.'

'Jeez man, it looks like he was shopping for his kids. Some sort of Star Wars toys or something.'

'What, you feel bad about that?'

'Yeah, kinda.'

'Oh. So, you feel bad about taking his Star Wars toys, but not about beating him up the side of the head with this,' his companion held up a short bat, 'Man, you're messed.'

'Sick,' the slight youth grinned, 'Anyway, my little brother will love this stuff.'

'You're a real sweetheart,' his companion laughed and slapped him on the shoulder. 'C'mon, let's go '

They ran off into the night, leaving the still form of Shiva Kiran lying on the ground, blood pooling beneath his ear, matting the long blonde hair.

Many hours later Shiva woke up, his head pounding. He pushed himself onto both hands, then reached for his communicator. He froze, as he realised it was gone. He patted his pockets and swore in a dozen languages. All of his equipment was gone including his laser gun. The side of his head felt sticky and he felt weak and dizzy. He stared at the pool of red blood on the ground.

He looked around, and pushed himself to his feet and stumbled along the street, knowing that he needed to get out of this district. Eventually he stumbled into an all-night fuel station and watched warily as people went in and out of a door marked with a small human figure. He decided to take a chance and walked in. There he found water, along with strange devices that seemed to be meant for people to relieve their bodily functions. They too, seemed to involve water. He watched as an older man came out of a cubicle dripping water. Shiva waited until the man had disappeared around the corner, then stepped closer to the cubicle and looked inside. Water was still dripping from a strange flower-like pipe in the wall over his head. Water planet, he reminded himself. It's a water planet. A younger man walked in the door and saw the blood down the side of Shiva's head and said something to him. Shiva without his translator, heard only gibberish, and stared blankly at the man. The man called out and a female entered the room and walked up to Shiva looking concerned. She asked something in the same gibberish, but when Shiva stared at her warily without answering, she took him carefully by the arm and led him out to a house at the back of the fuel station. She poured water over a cloth and he felt the sting as she cleaned up the side of his face. When she had finished, she made a clucking sound with her tongue and picked up what looked like a communications device. When blue flashing lights arrived at the front of the house, she went to the front door to let them in and Shiva made his escape out the back He slept that night in a tree, locking his arms tight around the branch. The next morning he felt a little better and left to find a better communications device. The one he had stolen from the woman did not work, it made strange noises at him at first, then went dead when he was only a few hundred metres from the house. He threw it away worried it might have had some sort of tracking device in it.

# CHAPTER TEN

M'Rel was in big silver sunglasses and a white beanie. With the same silvery blonde hair and fair skin as Laura, they could have been mistaken for sisters, which was just as well… Laura looked human, so people might assume M'Rel did too.

They wandered around the electronics store. Laura translated the labels on the equipment to M'Rel and explained as well as she could, how they worked.

'Damn it,' Laura heard a deep voice behind them exclaim.

The women ignored him, but then he came out with a stream of invectives that made Laura blush.

Forgetting that M'Rel couldn't understand him, Laura turned, irritated, 'Excuse me-' then she stopped.

Before her was the most amazing looking man she had ever seen. He had a powerful build and blonde wavy hair. His bare arms were muscular and tanned, and his face was strong and perfect. He glanced at her and their eyes locked, his an intense lapis blue, shaded by long, dark lashes and hers a sparkling silver-grey. Laura's heart skipped a beat, then another and she gasped at his graceful beauty.

She also remembered that it didn't matter how explicitly he swore, M'Rel wouldn't understand him. She didn't speak English.

But M'Rel had wandered off, her attention caught by a large electronic display further up the aisle.

'Do you speak,' Shiva asked, then stopped. He couldn't stop staring at Laura, taking in her fair skin, her silvery blonde hair, the sparkling silver eyes that seemed to see right through him.

'Hello,' she smiled, finding herself drawn to the tall man before her. 'What's the matter?'

'What do you mean?'

'You were swearing.'

'Oh, yes, I do apologize. I am looking for a communications device.'

'You mean one of these?' Laura asked, waving a hand at a glass display case full of mobile phones.

'Perhaps. How do they work?'

'You're kidding me, aren't you? You pick it up, dial the number and talk to them. It's not rocket science,' she smiled, shaking her head. So beautiful, so handsome, and so dumb.

'Pity,' he said and she stared at him.

'What?'

'What number? There are codes?'

'The phone number. What are you talking about? Everyone has a phone number,' she stared at him, wondering why she suddenly felt like she was talking to one of the Fey.

'Thank you. You have helped me more than you know,' he smiled, putting a hand on her arm in gratitude. If another man had done that, Laura would probably have put his head through the wall. But coming from this blue-eyed blonde Norse god, the gesture seemed so natural, so polite, that she simply smiled and nodded before continuing up the aisle.

Great, thought Laura, I get a chance to meet a real dreamboat just when I've met a bunch of people who will very probably be taking me off the planet in a few weeks. Laura looked back to the man and noticed him walking out of the shop. She sighed.

# CHAPTER ELEVEN

Laura, Trudi and M'Rel arrived back at the forestry in the old farm jeep and began lifting boxes from the back of the jeep.

Kinshah looked at them, his eyes lighting up and said, 'This much?'

'Would you believe, half of it is from toys,' Laura said and chuckled.

'This way,' Kinshah said, he led the group deeper into the forestry with their boxes. They walked for half an hour before Kinshah stopped beside a dense grove and pushed some bushes aside. Laura and Trudi saw the white curve of something which was obviously a ship's hull, protruding from deep underground.

Trudi ran her hands across the white surface and exclaimed, 'It's cold.'

Laura also put her hands on the hull and felt dust and grit fall away, leaving the surface pure white and silky under her touch.

'Kinshah, it's buried. How are you going to get it out?' Laura said.

'That will not be a problem once it is powered up,' Kinshah assured her, 'come, let us work.'

The Fey and the two girls all filed into the ship, through a small access hatch on the other side of the white hull. Inside the ship was pure white too, all curves and mysteriously lit up even though there were no windows.

Within several days, both Laura and Trudi were familiar with every part of the ship. Every day they drove the jeep up to the forestry and made the walk through the trees, then spent the day helping the Fey work.

Until one day, Kinshah surprised them by saying, 'It is done.'

'What do we do now?' Laura asked.

'Hopefully, we leave,' Kinshah answered.

Fifteen minutes later Laura and Trudi sat in awestruck delight as they felt the ship shift slightly beneath their chairs for the first time.

M'Rel called out from her chair, 'Power levels fluctuating, Kinshah, wait,'

'Controls fully responsive,' said the young man, De, to M'Rel's left. The other girl was called Binti, but she kept to herself and shared Kinshah's wary hostility towards Laura and Trudi.

'Power level waveforms damping to within acceptable limits, sir, but I wouldn't push her out too hard at this stage,' M'Rel warned.

'Do we have go for lift-off?' Kinshah asked, as though he did this every day of the week.

Maybe he did, thought Laura.

'Aye, sir,' M'Rel and Binti replied in unison.

'Lift off. Take us up to low planetary orbit.'

Trudi and Laura sat with huge eyes. The two chairs they were strapped into had high headrests with wings, like the rest of the seats along the back wall. The seatbelts they wore didn't seem adequate for what they were about to do, but M'Rel had assured them that the inertial dampers would ensure that they were not subjected to excessive G-forces in the ascent.

There was a sudden trilling hum and a layer of light appeared around the ship, apparently dissolving the dirt and mud and rocks around the ship, freeing it easily so that it swung loose and rose slowly. The view screen on the tiny ship lifted from its grassy resting place with a crunch of breaking grass roots. To Laura's surprise the view screen wrapped not only around to either side and up over the top of the front of the ship's hull, but underneath them as well, so it felt like they were sitting over nothing but open air. The light around the ship flared again and suddenly the view screen was free of mud, dust and plants.

Laura looked down past her feet at the ground below as the ship struggled up the first metre, then five metres, then suddenly fifty metres, then gasped as it looked like someone had sucked the Earth away from under their feet, until they were high enough to see the curve of the horizon and the blue haze over the Pacific Ocean to their East. The ocean now took up most of their view of the planet below them and though it had hardly felt as though they were moving, because of the inertial dampers, they must have travelled upwards about fifty thousand feet in only a few seconds. She had not expected their ascent to be so rapid.

Trudi leaned over to her and whispered, 'Close your mouth,' and Laura snapped her mouth shut. Trudi was grinning like a

Cheshire cat.

The view screen above their heads blackened and the stars came into view, even though it was not night. Laura gazed, entranced, at the brightness of the stars. Out here, she thought, the stars don't twinkle, they glow. She smiled and listened to the conversation of the Fey as it was translated by her mind into words and figures which were familiar to her.

'Have you calculated geostationary orbit for the planet, M'Rel?' Kinshah asked.

'Yes sir, 42,164 kilometres from planet's core.'

'Planet radius?' Kinshah asked.

'6,378 kilometres, sir.'

'Take us out to 35,786 kilometres from the surface,' he ordered.

A sudden pull and the Earth shrank, and Trudi and Laura stared down at the intense blue of Earth seen from space.

'Wow,' Laura said.

'Very wow,' Trudi added looking entranced.

'Sir, we are in geostationary orbit, but…' M'Rel looked puzzled.

'But what, M'Rel?'

'These power readings sir, they don't seem to be settling down.'

Kinshah unbuckled his seatbelt and walked over to M'Rel.

He studied the readouts and said, 'What the hell?'

He looked over the readings, reached over and punched a few buttons. A schematic appeared of the ship, with what looked like contour lines around it. The contour lines did not flow parallel around the outside of the ship's hull, though. There was a tiny circle where the control room would be on the ship, and the contour lines seemed to generate from that circle, only conforming themselves to the hull of the ship as they came out past the ship. The contour lines were *pulsing*. Every second, they contracted like an iris around the central circle, then relaxed again.

'Pinpoint that,' Kinshah said, pointing to the tiny circle, 'Is that within the ship?'

'Yes sir, localizing now,' but M'Rel was looking more and more incredulous as she turned and stared at Laura. 'Sir, the centre of the power fluctuations, is Laura.'

Kinshah looked at Laura and snapped, 'Double-check!'

'Aye sir,' Alien fingers flew over the board.

M'Rel looked back up at Kinshah. 'Confirmed, sir.'

'That's too big. No single person,' Kinshah stopped, stared

intently at Laura and nearly choked, 'unless-?'

Trudi recovered from her Earth-gazing to look around her and realised that something strange was happening by the frozen expression on the Fey's faces, 'What are they saying, Laura? What's wrong?'

Laura shook her head, 'I'm not sure.' She stared at Kinshah, worried by the look in his eyes. Why would she be the source of power fluctuations, and why was it worrying Kinshah so much? She hoped the Fey were not considering doing what Trudi had originally worried about. At the moment, looking at the terrified look in their eyes, she wasn't so sure they wouldn't shove them out of an airlock as soon as they got out of Earth's orbit.

'M'Rel?' Laura asked.

M'Rel stared at her and said quietly, 'We can easily achieve geostationary orbit and achieve hyperdrive with these power levels, sir. More than easily. The question is not whether we have enough power, it is whether we keep the fluctuations under control?'

Kinshah looked thoughtful, 'Can you use the medical scanners to lock in on that pulse rate and amplitude? If you could tie it in with the power dampers to compensate for the pulsation, that should give us a more stable baseline.'

'Excellent idea, sir,' M'Rel mumbled, her fingers again working their magic across the board before her, 'And done!'

The power levels stabilised. Laura felt the ship shudder and settle down around them.

'Do you think we could go into hyperdrive now?' Kinshah asked.

'Aye, sir, vessel secured and ready for drive,' M'Rel couldn't resist an anxious glance in Laura's direction.

'Track out to clear space, find us a launch point, M'Rel,' Kinshah directed and turned to Laura.

Laura eyed him warily, 'Would you mind telling me what's going on?'

'You appear to be the source of our power fluctuations,' Kinshah said.

'Me? I don't understand,' Laura said.

'Normal beings, are not the source of power fluctuations.' His voice was as cool as ever, but it was more respectful than it had been.

'So, I can make power fluctuations? That's abnormal?' Laura

asked.

'You are doing more than just causing fluctuations. You appear to be generating a great deal of power,' he replied.

'What, so, I'm a human generator now?' Laura shot Trudi a look which said, *'Oh, please….'*

Trudi sat silently, looking concerned. She had seen enough of the Fey's reactions and heard enough of Laura's responses to realise most of what was going on. She spoke up, 'Hear him out, Laura. See what he has to say. It might be important.'

Kinshah said, 'Not human, definitely not human.'

Laura's eyes skated over to him, then to Trudi, then back to him.

'What then?' she asked.

'A powerful operant. A hybrid, I'm guessing, only you are too powerful. You must be,'

'Operant? Operant of what?'

Kinshah stared at her, 'Anything you like, I would guess, looking at these readings.'

'But I don't understand. What do you mean by 'operant'? What can I do?'

'Anything,' M'Rel whispered, tapping her readout and looking worried.

Kinshah looked back over his shoulders at the readouts and froze. They had just passed the moon, which was starting to shrink gradually in the viewer.

'The further we get from the suppression generator, the more powerful the readings sir.'

'Holy…' Kinshah said and looked at Laura. This time he didn't just look terrified, he looked like death warmed over and like he wished he had been a hell of a lot nicer to Laura from the beginning.

'Suppression generator?' Laura asked, intrigued.

'She does not know of this,' observed the young helmsman, De.

'Damned Union!' Kinshah said and took Laura by the arm. He pointed at the lower end of the moon. Just catching the light reflected from Earth as they moved past it rapidly, Laura could see what looked like the top of some sort of domed structure, almost hidden, buried at the south pole of the Moon. 'See that? That is what keeps you humans on Earth; the suppression generator. It was placed there four thousand years ago, so that the Union could use this as a prison planet for intractable humans.'

Laura looked puzzled, 'Suppression generator? Isn't that a contradiction in terms? Does it suppress, or generate?'

De explained, 'It generates a field, the effect of which is to suppress all activity within the space-time continuum, including psychic abilities. You humans are even better than the Fey at things psychic.'

Laura was shaking her head, 'So what, wait, we're prisoners? But we haven't done anything wrong!'

'Not you, your ancestors. You are just the dangerous descendants, of a dangerous race of people, banished to this hell-hole for the sins of your fathers.'

'What did we do? I mean, what did our ancestors do?' Laura asked.

'What didn't they do? Blew up the moon of the Elves for one thing,' Kinshah replied.

'Fought with the Fey,' De said.

'Wiped out the Djinn' M'Rel added.

'Hunted down every last Unichron and slaughtered them,' Kinshah said.

'Shall we go on?' M'Rel asked.

Laura stared at her and Kinshah, 'You're telling me that this planet of ours, Earth, is a prison planet? And that life sentence is not enough, they include all our descendants? For how long, forever? What happens when humans develop space travel in their own right and start exploring out there?'

'Ah, that is not likely,' Kinshah said.

'What do you mean?' Laura asked.

'The suppression generator suppresses human psychic abilities, but it also decreases the ability of any mechanical device, such as a ship, to warp space or time and to skip between realities. Also, without your psychic powers, you humans can't get your minds working together, so that it becomes unlikely that you will develop the sort of intellectual cooperation and information sharing required to develop the science required for viable space travel,' Kinshah said.

'But how is your ship operating, then?' Laura asked.

'Look at our power utilisation curve,' M'Rel explained. 'We are using far more power than we normally would to achieve space-lift, this is to compensate for the effect of the suppression generator.

Fortunately, with you aboard, we have far more power available than normal. You,' she hesitated as Kinshah shook his head slightly at her, 'are a very powerful operative,' she finished in a vague manner.

Laura glared at them and returned to her survey of the moon and Earth disappearing rapidly behind them. She was losing the ability to concentrate on what Kinshah and M'Rel were saying because her hands were starting to feel odd. They felt like there was a flow around them, some sort of magnetic tugging current, like warm water was flowing around her hands, only she could control the flow. She lifted her hands before her and felt them pulsing with power.

Laura reached out to touch the console before her and the console lights flowed around her hand at it passed them, distorting like candles in a breeze as her hand passed by. Laura was entranced and felt strange instincts and knowledge, start to flow into her mind. She realised that she could feel the minds around her, just as she could feel the flow of the space-time continuum around her bare hands. Laura sat in a nexus of currents of space and time and thoughts, and remembered crash landing in the escape pod as a baby, the last time her hands had swept easily through the space-time continuum and shaped it to her needs.

Laura saw Trudi watching her, looking worried. Laura stared at her hands like they were brand new, and wondered whether Trudi could also feel the lessening of the effect of the suppression generator as they moved slowly out away from the moon.

As the moon shrank Laura saw M'Rel watching her warily. Laura did not feel hostility towards the Fey, but began to feel anger building within her as she thought about her race being imprisoned like common criminals. Laura could feel her powers steadily building up as they departed the suppression field. She felt a rush of anger as she thought about her planet and her people, helpless and incarcerated behind her.

The Fey ship lurched and lurched again before swinging back the way they had come. Laura asked De coldly, 'What's the range and power of your weapons?'

De stared at her blankly and Laura prompted, 'From how far out could they destroy that suppression generator?'

De was shaking his head, but found himself answering against his will, 'Easily, from here,' he fell forwards as the ship lurched to a sudden halt from near-light speed.

M'Rel screamed as she felt the power of Laura's mind crawling around inside her skull, extracting weapons information from her. The ship hummed as the weapons generators charged, swung around and steadied, facing the dark side of the moon. Abruptly, seven powerful blue bubbles of energy left the ship.

M'Rel screamed, 'No!' as the torpedoes headed for the south pole of the moon and the suppression generator.

'Damn your prison planet,' Laura growled as the immobilised Fey stood helpless in her psychic grip. There was blackness and silence for several more seconds, then a batch of white circles swelled on the surface of the moon, as the suppression generator exploded in a spectacular fireworks display. The sound having no atmosphere to vibrate through was never created and did not reach their ears through the vacuum of space.

There was a long, terrible silence, then the Fey felt the vice-grip on their minds being released.

'My God, what have you done?' Kinshah said, leaning forward over the front of his chair, his knuckles white.

'What any decent person would have done. I freed my people. I thought you didn't approve of the Galactic Union?'

'But you will release the Terrans on the galaxy!' he said.

'Damn right I will and you would do the same if it were your people!' Laura looked at them coldly and asked, 'Now, I have a question for the Fey. Are you with us, or against us?'

'We cannot speak for the rest of the Fey,' Kinshah said.

'Yeah, well, maybe you'd better find me someone who can.'

Kinshah stared at her, horrified.

Two hundred light years away, Domhan Keallach sat bolt upright in his bunk and whispered, 'Anail de mo anam!'

He dressed quickly and headed for the bridge of his ship at a run. The twin-bond had leapt to life in his mind and he sensed the unmistakeable mind-print of his sister.

'Sir,' the communications officer said, 'We have some unusual activity in the buffer zone around the planet Earth. Some explosions, several ships in transit and some strange energy readings.'

'Set a course for it, full hyperdrive now,' Domhan ordered and hit the alert button on his chair arm to wake up his prime shift. He coded in the course bearings himself with swift fingers, without the need of the sensors to tell him coordinates.

Domhan Keallach was smiling for the first time in twenty-two years.

# CHAPTER TWELVE

On the massive Reingold, Zokar Rizian was staring transfixed and horrified, as he watched the suppression generator blown to smithereens on his view screen, 'Shields at maximum power. Where's that fire coming from?' He strode down to stand behind the helm and weapons consoles.

'Further out sir, near the next planet, but it's too far off and it's moving fast. We can't pinpoint it.'

'Watch for incoming. Check long-range scanners. Deploy defensive mines around ship and hold them to us with a low level tractor beam. Hold our position, but charge hyperdrive. If we come under attack I want us around the other side of Earth before you blink, helm.'

The helm and navigation officers were tight lipped, their fingers flying over their consoles as they tried to keep up with the rapid-fire orders coming from Zokar.

'I don't think we've been targeted sir, no incoming missiles. Scanners find no weapons locked on us. We can't scan the other ship, they're too far away. I'm pretty sure they are just targeting the generator.'

'Pretty sure, but we can't be totally sure. Stay on top of it,' Zokar joined his lieutenant at the scanning station, ran twelve slender, expert fingers over the boards and was satisfied, 'We're okay for now, but that doesn't mean that once the dust clears we won't become a target'

'But sir,' the helmsman, a junior officer spoke, 'We're rigged for silent running, we're fully cloaked.'

'And they have just demonstrated weaponry far advanced of ours, helmsman. Who's to say their scanners aren't far superior also? They are probably watching us as we speak. You don't think I would have broken silent running by putting out defensive mines unless I thought we were already visible, do you?'

The scanning tech smiled. He knew better than to question Zokar's orders and the young helmsman looked abashed, 'Sorry, sir.'

Zokar walked over beside him, 'Helmsman, I do not object to questions such as yours. As long as it *never* extends to disobeying orders, it is not a problem. And your adherence to orders is unquestioned.'

'Thank you, sir.' But the helmsman was wary. He had seen Zokar Rizian shoot a man for insubordination. The elf had pulled out his laser and shot him as quietly and efficiently as he was directing and encouraging his staff now. However that insubordination had cost one crewman, and almost Captain Kiran his life.

Zokar focused on the scenario playing out before them, leaving part of his mind focused on keeping the young crew calm and running efficiently. He knew they were terrified of him but that meant he had to reassure them occasionally to maintain their performance at peak efficiency.

Zokar looked thoughtful and said, 'Just in case, notch up our speed and duck around darkside, then stay on the other side of the Earth to the original source of those torpedoes.'

The helmsman did as he was told, then looked enquiringly at Zokar.

Zokar smiled, and said, 'No harm in having a planet between us and the enemy, ensign.' Then his face dropped to a more serious expression and he said, 'The next problem is, how do we get our people on the surface out safely?'

He thought of Shiva, isolated with a few security guards, on a planet full of savages. Savages who without the suppression generator would realise their abilities and start to flex their psychic muscles. Zokar shivered and began to pace the bridge anxiously.

Laura stared at the massive black and red Reingold until it passed out of view behind Earth. She was in a spaceship, she was out in space. Why did her mind do such a backflip to see another spaceship orbiting Earth?

'Who are they? I thought you said this planet was forbidden?' she asked Kinshah.

He turned to her from the scanners before him, 'It looks like a Galactic Trade Alliance ship. They must have been rigged for silent running, but we disturbed them and they broke out of silent running to ramp up their defences. They ducked around the back of the planet when we blew up the generator. Maybe they're just hoping to stay out of harm's way. They certainly aren't acting aggressive.'

'But what are they doing here?' she walked up to peer over his shoulder.

'Unknown. It is unusual. They know about the Union's ban on this planet. That's a big ship, it would cost a lot of money to bring that out here and Traders don't waste money.'

'Why don't we go ask them?'

'They may feel obliged to defend themselves, if we chase them. Although their weapons are primitive by our standards, once we get into close range the sheer volume that one of those Trader ships carries could be a real problem for us. I would advise against it,' Kinshah straightened up from the scanners and leant back against the console behind him, folding his arms.

'Yes, but it's not your planet they're circling like a bunch of vultures, is it Kinshah? I'm taking us in closer for a look-see. These Galactic Trader types, do you think they'd be up for a discussion?'

'If they think there's money in it for them, absolutely,' Kinshah said.

'Do we have anything that's worth money to them?' Laura asked.

'Not really,' he said.

But Laura was looking over his shoulder at the rear scanners and said, torn between worry and satisfaction, 'Yeah we do.'

'What?' Kinshah said puzzled and turned around.

'Safe passage. Look on the rear scanners.' She pointed at another screen which showed the aft view from their ship.

Kinshah and M'Rel looked and saw on the scanners; four enormous Union Battle Cruisers closing in rapidly from behind them, The hyperdrive wash surrounding the Union ships would be forcing them to hold their shields up and prevent them from detecting the Fey ship.

Kinshah yelled at Laura, 'Get us behind your planet, now.'

The Fey ship lurched, but spun around and whipped around behind the planet nearly colliding with the Reingold, which broke silence.

'Galactic Trade Alliance vessel Reingold here. We are fully armed and prepared for battle. Any hostilities will be met with immediate and deadly force.'

M'Rel glanced quickly up at the view screen, which now showed a tall pale-haired elf with icy silver eyes and snapped, 'Save your breath. Four Union Battle Cruisers just showed up on the other side of Earth. We're ducking behind the hedge too.'

Zokar Rizian stared at the silvery blonde girl on his screen with the neat triangular face and the silver eyes. She was stunning in an exotic way. Too exotic, he realised. 'You are Fey. What are you doing near Earth?'

'We could ask you the same question elf,' M'Rel said.

'We are attempting a rescue mission. Our captain and many of our crew are stranded down there.'

'Pull the other one, Trader. What were they doing down there in the first place?'

'And what is your mission on Earth?' The response was laced with sarcasm, 'Sabotage?' He put his hands on his hips.

'Mission?' Laura stepped in to view on his screen, 'I have no mission. I was born here. The Fey were shipwrecked here.'

Zokar stopped, staring at the second silver haired woman. Was she Fey, or Human? He went to speak, stopped, then stared at her for several seconds before shaking himself mentally and answering her brusquely, 'You have just committed an act of galactic terrorism the likes of which has never been seen. You have destroyed the suppression generator which keeps the entire civilised galaxy safe from the Terran menace. Why should we not blow you out of space right now?'

''The Terran menace'?' Laura snarled at him, 'You won't blow us out of space because you can't. You don't have the weaponry and if you did try those Union Battle Cruisers would scan the energy surges and probably blow you out of space.'

'How does she know that?' Kinshah asked M'Rel quietly, looking agitated.

'Shhhhhh, she's picking up everything we think and know and there's not a damned thing we can do about it,' M'Rel murmured.

'What did you say?' Zokar Rizian asked looking past Laura at the whispering Fey. They both mutely shook their heads and looked to Laura.

'In any case, the Union vessels know we're here,' continued Zokar, 'You have seen to that.'

Laura pointed out, 'They know we're here. They don't know

you're here. If you want it kept that way follow us.'

Zokar tilted his head ruefully. She was right, the Union ships had not scanned the Reingold before they came out of hyperdrive. The Fey ship turned on a path directly away from Earth, perpendicular to the orbital position of the Union ships' approach, keeping Earth between them and the four battle cruisers.

'Sir?' asked the helmsman.

'Hold your position, helm, we're not going anywhere,' Zokar grumbled.

Something was bugging Zokar about the conversation they had just had, he leaned forward, hit the communications unit again, 'Wait.'

'What?' The Fey ship slowed to a near-stop. Laura was controlling it and the Fey, now, without really noticing. The Fey noticed, though. Their hands and minds would only do certain things. If they tried to go against Laura's will, their hands simply would not move and their minds went blank.

'Did you say you were born on Earth? But you are Fey.'

'She's part human,' offered M'Rel. She hadn't taken her wary eyes off Zokar Rizian since his face had appeared on her view screen.

'And part elf, I bet,' Zokar added, looking at the delicately upturned eyebrows. Laura didn't have pointed ears, but somehow... he switched off the communications unit and said to Elesk, 'Scan that Fey ship. What life forms does it show?'

'Four Fey, one human, one...'she looked hesitant, 'mixed race, looks like an illegal hybrid, there's more sir, it's showing as a three-way mix of Human, Elven and Fey, highly illegal; a tribred!' her voice was thick with disapproval, but a small light appeared on her sensor array and began beeping urgently. Elesk stared at it and looked at Zokar with wide eyes.

Even Zokar Rizian froze for several seconds. He regained his wits long moments before the younger members of his crew though. 'I got it,' he murmured to his cousin, then switched the communications unit back on and said, 'Fey ship, surrender your passenger immediately or we will blast you out of space!'

Laura looked at M'Rel with a frown, 'Was it something I said? They don't like hybrids? Anyway, can he do that?'

M'Rel pursed her lips, 'Unless you're sure you can stop him, I wouldn't take the chance. At this range, they do have quite an arsenal of weapons. The question is, why does he want you?'

'She's hybrid, they may simply wish to execute her,' Kinshah said hopefully.

M'Rel, Trudi and Laura all shot him dirty looks. He shrugged innocently.

'Oh great,' Laura exclaimed and glared at the screen. Then she thought to ask, 'Could they? If I got over there, could they kill me?'

M'Rel and Kinshah looked at each other, 'Probably not, from what we have seen of your abilities,' Kinshah said.

'Probably not, you're not sure,' Laura said.

'Well, the suppression field has been destroyed. There should be no constraints on your natural abilities now. Their only hope would be to take you unawares,' Kinshah said.

Laura considered her situation. It didn't take much pondering to realise she and Trudi would be safer on board the Galactic Trader Vessel than aboard the tiny half-wrecked Fey ship with a crew of only four. If it came to the pinch, the Reingold offered a much greater fuel supply and a greater range of travel, also more places to hide on-board if it came to stowing away. There was just the slightest doubt about whether she could control the bigger ship and greater number of crewmembers on the Reingold. She decided to take the chance.

'Agree to the surrender,' Laura said.

'Gladly,' Kinshah growled. He wanted control of his ship back and to do that required getting Laura off the ship.

'Galactic Trader, we seek assurances that our passenger will not be harmed,' M'Rel warned on the comm. Kinshah glared at her, annoyed at the delay. He wanted Laura off his ship and he wanted to flee this brewing battle.

Zokar scratched an ear thoughtfully. He doubted very much whether he and his crew could harm the silver tribred, if she was who they thought she was, 'Very well. If she does not suit our purposes she will be sent back to you unharmed.' It was a cool elvish lie.

Laura leaned forward and said, 'What is your name?'

'Zokar Rizian.'

'Will you guarantee the safety of this ship and the Fey once I'm off it?' Laura asked.

Zokar tilted his head, smiled and sighed, caught out. He decided it was not profitable to dissemble at this point. They didn't have time for a long argument, with the four Union ships closing in from behind Earth, 'Probably not. Their knowledge of our existence jeopardises my entire crew. They could reveal us to the Union ships at any time, then escape.'

'You have an odd sense of humour, Zokar Rizian, if that thought makes you smile,' Laura commented icily. She didn't trust the tall silver-haired humanoid with the exotic features.

'I am smiling because I have a question for you. How did you know to ask that question?'

'What does he mean?' Laura asked M'Rel.

'He seems to be asking how you know that *you* are more important to them than possession of a technologically advanced spaceship and fully trained crew.' M'Rel was glaring at Zokar, realising just how close the Fey had come to being incinerated by the elf with no more thought than one swats a bug.

Laura gave her a long look, then turned to Zokar, 'Call it a gut instinct,' she smiled, 'Will you guarantee their safety?'

'I guarantee their safety from our ship provided they show no hostility.' Zokar said.

'Laura, the word of an elf, when you are at cross purposes with him.' M'Rel murmured.

'Is worth jack shit?' Laura asked softly, and M'Rel nodded. Laura smiled coldly, 'I kind of guessed that,' she whispered, then turned back to the view screen, 'We'll wait, I think,' Laura said, 'you won't fire on this ship while I'm on it.'

Zokar Rizian glared at the tribred, frustrated. Until he had her aboard his ship and under control, he could not retrieve Shiva Kiran from the planet's surface and escape from the Union fleet on the other side of the planet.

Kinshah glared at Laura, too. He wanted her off this ship and he wanted to get away from Earth.

But M'Rel looked at Laura thoughtfully, then asked Trudi quietly, 'Why does she not go? The other ship is safer for her. The Union ships will be loath to fire on a Galactic Trade Alliance ship.'

'She is concerned for your safety,' Trudi explained.

M'Rel blinked and looked at Laura with the beginnings of admiration in her Fey eyes.

Zokar Rizian was growing puzzled. What were the Union ships doing? Normally they would have settled into orbit by now and the Reingold and the Fey ship would have been detected and had to flee.

'Why haven't those Union ships appeared in orbit yet?' he wondered out loud.

'I don't know,' Kinshah said, 'and I don't care. Let's just get out of here.'

'No,' Zokar declared flatly.

Laura remembered that he had told them his captain was down there with some of their crew. The captain must have some hold over this cold-eyed, evasive creature, she realised. Otherwise Zokar would have cut and run, without the Fey ship or Laura, simply for the sake of self-preservation. She knew without needing instinct that the Reingold, although massive and bristling with weaponry, was no match for the four grey behemoths on the other side of Earth. She had seen in M'Rel's mind how massive the ships had to be to make the scanner signatures which they had.

'So, you are waiting for this captain of yours,' Laura said, fishing for information. She earned herself a glittering glare from the silver eyes of the elf.

'But he's right,' puzzled Kinshah, 'What are the Union ships doing?'

'Could they be in trouble?' M'Rel asked.

'They couldn't be a threat to Earth, could they?' Laura said worried. Zokar had referred to the 'Terran menace', what if the Union ships had arrived to find the suppression generator gone and the menace threatening to run loose about the galaxy. What might they do?

'Let's sneak a look around the other side of Earth,' Laura suggested, part of her mind anxious, but another part still unable to believe that she could say that and have the people around her take her seriously.

'We cannot take on four Union Battle Cruisers, Laura. I'm taking this ship out of here,' Kinshah said, 'I did not go to all this trouble to save my crew and then get them blown up in battle. We are going home. Go with this Galactic Trader if you wish to stay here on Earth.'

Laura bit her lip, then said to Zokar Rizian, 'You heard him. You want me. Let me and Trudi come across and let the Fey go. They have done nothing wrong.'

Zokar was quiet, then nodded, 'You have my word.'

M'Rel pulled Laura aside, 'Why the sudden change of heart? He is still an elf. You cannot trust him.'

'I don't have to trust him. I can read his mind.'

M'Rel's eyes went wide, 'From here? What are you, that you can do these things?'

'I don't know, M'Rel. I do know that I must stay and protect Earth. And this elf is too worried about his captain and crew down on Earth to be concerned with killing you. You'd better leave quickly, though, or he may change his mind'

'M'Rel!' Kinshah said, uncomfortable by the whispering between the two women.

'I have to go with them. They cannot pilot this ship home without me,' M'Rel explained, 'But I will come back to you.'

'There is no need, M'Rel. Go home to your people,' Laura said.

M'Rel blinked at her, then nodded and returned to her console.

Laura said, 'You can send the shuttle now, Zokar.'

Laura collected Trudi with a touch to the arm as she left and they went to the back of the ship to wait at the airlock for the shuttle. It arrived at the Fey ship in a surprisingly short amount of time. The airlock opened, and six black-shirted guards stepped out of the shuttle and walked over to Laura and Trudi on the hangar deck, then arranged themselves in a circle around them.

Laura hesitated and asked the nearest one wryly, 'Expecting trouble from me?'

To her surprise the burly guard stared at her, then realised what he had done and averted his gaze downwards. He began to shake like a leaf before kneeling and whispered, 'No, O Most High,'

She frowned and looked at the rest of them, which had the interesting effect of them all shuffling back from her, eyes averted downwards, then dropping to their knees, some even planted their faces on the floor.

Laura shook her head, smiling and said wryly, 'Great.'

As Laura and Trudi stepped over the prone guards and forward towards the shuttle, Trudi commented dryly, 'I hope to hell they're not our bodyguards. Come on, get your faces off the deck and look alert. Let's go!'

The guards stood nervously and surrounded the two young women as they turned to the shuttle door. Not one of them was under six foot and it was hard to see out past them.

Trudi and Laura watched, transfixed, as the shuttle took them away from the smaller Fey ship and towards the Galactic Trade

Ship. It felt surreal to be out here, in space, on a shuttle between two space ships. Laura had pinch-marks up her arm where she had pinched herself to ensure that she wasn't dreaming.

The shuttle fed in through the shuttle bay doors of the Galactic Trade Ship and after the bay doors shut behind them they heard a hiss which they assumed was pressure equalizing, but the hiss continued too long and the burly guards collapsed around them as darkness also claimed them.

'Cowards,' Zokar muttered under his breath as he watched the Fey ship leave.

Still, it was one less variable for him to contend with. The Fey were notoriously fickle and he did not want to risk them turning on him. He turned his thoughts to the four Union ships that were approaching the planet. They had arrived uncloaked, so they must be here on legitimate Union business. Was that business following the Reingold? He hoped not, for that would imply that news of the Reingold's quest out here at Earth had leaked back to the Union.

'Brig, are the prisoners secured and unconscious?' Zokar asked into his communications panel.

'Aye, sir,' came the response.

# CHAPTER THIRTEEN

Curiosity; to some people it's a mild emotion. To others it burns more brightly. To a rare few, it's like an internal fire that is never switched off. And it's surprising how many of those rare few end up in the space program.

Chin Li stood glued to the window of the space station with the other occupants and stared entranced at the scenario played out before them. First the stars in front of them had wobbled, much as they might on a hazy night on the marshland below his mountain home. But there was no atmosphere in the vacuum of space, so there should be no atmospheric effects, like wobbling. Chin had called his compatriots over to the viewing window and stared as the mysterious wobbliness took up the whole star field, then the stars seemed to stabilise again.

But suddenly seven beams of light shot from out near Mars towards the moon above them and a massive white explosion rocked the far side of the moon. Then an amazing white spaceship swung towards them, all curves and streamlining. He stared stunned and wondered if he was dreaming. Then a very pragmatic thought came to his mind, why would you need streamlining in space?

The white ship swung away and disappeared behind Earth.

'International Space Station to Beijing Base!' Chin didn't realise he was yelling, he stopped, because he saw the behemoths. There were four of them. They were large and grey, like great grey aircraft carriers or battleships, only fifty times bigger. They had come from nowhere and were heading steadily towards Earth.

'Beijing! International Space Station here. We appear to have an influx of large alien vessels on our hands!'

That ought to get their attention, thought Chin Li.

The curiosity in Chin's mind was flaring like magnesium now, as he checked that every recording device on the space station was on and that the only transmission equipment operating was the transmitter back to base.

A reply came through from Earth, 'Base, ah, Major, how do you know they're, ah, 'alien vessels'?'

The base lieutenant was clearly thinking that Chin Li had gone irrevocably space-happy.

'Video streaming should be coming through to you now, Lieutenant.'

'Sir, yes Sir, coming through loud and clear!' the young lieutenant was rattled when the images of the ships came up on his computer screen. The footage was set against the usual backdrop from the space station and was so real that the lieutenant knew that this was not a set-up by his colleagues.

Within minutes, the only image on television news feeds across the globe was of the four huge ships and the occasional brief footage of the Fey ship as it swung past the space station towards the other side of Earth from the battle cruisers.

Newscasters in the absence of any further information were indulging in wild and constant speculation about the presence of the five ships.

Normally the inhabitants of the blue-green jewel of a planet would be captivated by such a story, but today they were not.

Today they had their own problems.

# CHAPTER FOURTEEN

The suppression generator on Earth's oversized moon had sapped the humans on Terra of their energies and psychic abilities for millennia, frustrating them, psychically blinding them, and shortening their lifespans to a few short decades. However, when a slave is strapped to a heavy grinding wheel his physical muscles grow incredibly strong over the years and the humans living under the dampening effect of the suppression generator had unconsciously been flexing their psychic muscles against its restrictive effect all their lives.

When that restrictive effect was removed, the psychic chains around the humans disappeared.

Shiva strolled down the street and saw a small child trip and stub his toe. He fell to the ground crying and Shiva watched as people around the child gasped in pain. Several of them sat down and grabbed their own toes, looking perplexed. Shiva expected his own foot to start hurting, but it did not.

As Shiva strolled further a small toy floated towards him He heard a small excited voice and a small girl ran towards him calling, 'Mummy, mummy, come and look at my lego helicopter. It's flying!' The helicopter swooped low towards a kitten in a front yard and the kitten took off, running up a tree, yowling with fear.

A smaller human sat in the front yard and looked up at the kitten. The small boy held up a hand and the kitten floated from the branch, meowing plaintively. Its claws outstretched and paddled thin air until it landed gently in front of the smaller human. Shiva started to nibble his bottom lip and glanced upwards at the sky. Where were the shuttles? Why hadn't Zokar come for him? What was happening to the humans around him? He tried to use his mind to lift a small rock up from the ground, but nothing happened.

He walked on, came to a busy intersection and hesitated. Crossing roads with ground traffic was a skill that Shiva had almost forgotten, so he hung back with the small crowd on the corner, waiting for them to walk across.

A young woman with a pram stood next to Shiva. She was talking on a communications device and waited for a gap in the traffic, then pushed the pram hastily out before her. The wheel got caught in a crack on the edge of the pavement and she shoved at it, then walked out across the road not seeing the oncoming truck until the last minute.

She screamed and froze over the pram, throwing her hands up as if to stop the truck.

Shiva closed his eyes, realising it was too late to do anything, and not wanting to see the tragedy unfolding before him.

Silence? Shiva realised his eyes were still closed and opened them. A large shadow was flickering over his head. Above them all, slices of the truck shuffled like cards up and over the woman and the pram, then seemed to stretch out like an accordion above her head, then shuffled back down on the other side of the woman and reassembled themselves back into the shape of the truck, which moved on in slow motion, in absolute silence. The woman snatched the baby and ran to the pavement, clutching the baby protectively. The woman had run back to stand next to Shiva and was shaking.

The untouched empty pram was still sitting in the middle of the road and some illogical impulse made her move towards it again, but Shiva placed a restraining hand on her arm. Another truck obliterated the pram in front of them and continued on, brakes smoking and smashed silently into a light pole on the corner of the intersection. Sound returned to the world around Shiva and his ears were assaulted with the sounds of metal screeching across tarmac, the baby crying and the woman screaming and screaming beside him until her voice became hoarse. She ran away up the footpath, clutching her child. Above them all, the driver of the second truck hovered unharmed, enveloped in a white, soft glow.

Shiva crossed the street and found himself behind two youths, who were walking quickly along.

'He's down here. I just know he is!' the younger one said and started running towards the next corner where several large bins of rubbish were lined up along the footpath.

A small, filthy, white dog emerged from under the bins, wagging its tail furiously. It ran up to the boys.

The older one cried out in delight, 'Leo!' and gathered the small dirty bundle in his arms. He looked at his younger friend and asked, 'How did you know where he was? It's been four days.'

'I don't know. I just knew. All of a sudden, I just knew.'

Shiva walked past them and tried to feel outwards with his mind, but he could detect nothing. He sighed, and wondered just how powerful the humans around him had become, living under the suppression generator. Time would tell, he supposed.

A gravelly voice beside him made him jump, 'Hey, man.'

Shiva turned, his hand going to his disruptor with lightning speed, but he didn't have a disruptor. He looked at the four tall men who had surrounded him and realised that once again, he had walked into a dangerous situation whilst preoccupied with observing the humans around him. He stopped moving and watched the humans as they approached. One slipped a large knife from under his shirt and the other three smiled nastily at him.

Shiva dropped his weight into his hips and waited confidently, he knew they didn't have a hope. After all, there were only four of them. But then he tried to move his hands and found them frozen by some unnameable force. One of the four men was gazing intently at him and Shiva got the impression that his sudden immobility was a result of that gaze.

A cold pit of fear began to form in Shiva's stomach, as the man with the knife stepped up to him, smiled sweetly and thrust the knife up against Shiva's throat, pricking the skin. Shiva tried to squirm away but couldn't. He could not even blink and his eyes began to feel dry.

Then all four of his attackers were lifted off the ground by about a metre and started yelling in protest.

A female voice behind Shiva said quietly, 'That's not very nice, boys.'

Shiva found he could move again and turned gratefully to his rescuer, a beautiful dark-skinned woman with liquid brown eyes.

She said to him, 'I think you'd better get out of here. I can handle this lot. I actually have a score or two to settle with them.'

Shiva nodded thankfully and sprinted away. The humans around him were becoming more and more dangerous by the second and it was rapidly turning into a dog-eat-dog situation where the most powerful psychic ruled. Shiva realised that a township might not be the best place for him. He found his way onto the back of farmer's utility truck and relaxed a little as it headed out of the city.

Back on the Reingold, Zokar was nervous. He walked over to Elesk's scanning station and asked, 'Anything?'

'Sir, I can't locate Captain Kiran's communicator, and without that we can't find him.'

Zokar grunted, then pointed at her view screen, 'What's happening there?'

On the viewer, which was scanning Earth in a seemingly random manner, a small wooden boat had appeared, floundering in high seas and obviously sinking. But in the middle of the deck, a small figure held out both hands and before it a wall of water about two metres high had frozen into rolling impotence at the edge of the boat.

'Change the view. Get audio' Zokar said.

Elesk complied and they heard the voice of the small Terran child over the raging storm, yelling frantically, 'Daddy, if I can do this, you can stop the storm.'

A taller figure, ragged and skinny, stepped up beside the child and held up his arms, lowered his head and closed his eyes.

'What's he doing?' Elesk asked.

'Shh.'

Zokar watched the viewer, enthralled, as they saw the sea around the boat slowly become calm. In a matter of seconds a circle of flat water stretched for two hundred metres around the boat in every direction. Beyond that calm circle with the tiny boat in the centre, the sea raged on unabated.

The boat's captain and his motley crew hastily began repairing the holes in the wooden hull, with boards and rope and wax, all the while staring at their saviours.

Elesk looked up at Zokar, 'If that is what a small child can now do,'

'Then they are dangerous indeed,' Zokar said. It did nothing to quell                    his                    anxiety.

# CHAPTER FIFTEEN

The first two Galactic Union ships had remained in hyperdrive too long to prevent disaster. The navigators on the two lead ships had calculated precisely how long they needed to stay in hyperdrive to power them ahead of the two rear ships, through the dampening field of the suppression generator and into close proximity to Earth. This involved staying in hyperdrive just a few nanoseconds longer than the two rear ships.

With the destruction of the suppression generator that dampening field was removed. The leading two ships were suddenly travelling through hyperspace without the resistance they expected and overshot their planned destination.

The truck driver looked in his rear view mirror, said something and hit the brakes, sending Shiva tumbling amongst a full load of pumpkins, adding a couple more bruises to his tally.

The driver jumped from his truck and pointed up in the sky behind Shiva and said, 'What the hell is that, man?'

Shiva stared at him. He understood him. Was he getting some of the abilities of the Terrans, or were the Terrans getting so much more powerful now that their thoughts projected clearly to anyone around them?

The driver grabbed his arm and pointed, 'Look!'

Shiva looked behind them and saw a strange swirling in the atmosphere above, as though the air were caught in a whirlpool of distortion. Shiva frowned.

Several other cars had pulled up behind them and people were getting out, some just cursing the driver of Shiva's truck for stopping, but others following Shiva and the driver's gazes behind them and up.

Above them, a sudden subsonic bass note sounded, so low that it took several seconds for the humans to hear it. They felt it in their spines, their bladders, and their bleeding noses.

After the boom and the screams from behind them, the driver

looked down, because a thick silver chain that he wore around his neck was floating upwards. He grabbed at it, but all he managed to do was dislodge it and it flew up into the air. Everyone around them was experiencing the same phenomenon. A tool kit flew upwards from the tray of the truck. In a radius of about two kilometres, every small piece of metal that was not bolted down had lifted into the air and floated, forming an unsteady, giant donut of metal pieces, revolving around the centre of the strange swirling in the atmosphere behind them.

Shiva grabbed the driver and yelled at the other people, 'Take cover!' He leapt into the ditch at the side of the road, dragging the cursing driver with him.

Above them the floating metal leapt and swirled around a building core of white light, from which a Galactic Union battle cruiser emerged and crashed to the ground in the blink of an eye.

The white core exploded with a crack, then a deep shudder and everything on the ground was shattered and lifted upwards, for miles in every direction. In the ditch, the driver and Shiva looked up in horror, expecting dead bodies all along the road after the violence of the explosion. But each and every person stood, unharmed but perplexed, surrounded by an aura of soft white light, amid the endless destruction. Shiva stared at his body and saw the same light and realised that the truck driver was the source of his protection. They had been lying together when the wave of destruction hit and the driver's aura had engulfed Shiva too.

Several Terrans had started walking back towards town and one of them lifted up and floated along before others followed.

Shiva started walking along the road out of town heading towards the dark forestry a few miles ahead of him. There would be shelter in there and trees to fashion crude weapons. He looked behind him to the floating humans and decided the wilderness was safer than staying in contact with the Terrans and their developing psychic powers. He had been on the receiving end of those powers and knew he could not stand against a hostile Terran human for long.

He pondered his own seeming complete lack of psychic ability. He sighed, cursing the irony of it. He, Shiva Kiran, warrior and leader, the best fighter in the quadrant reduced by his lack of psychic ability to running away and hiding. He had no choice, even a    Terran    child    was    more    powerful    than    him.

# CHAPTER SIXTEEN

The second Galactic Union battle cruiser dropped out of hyperdrive just outside Earth's atmosphere. The ship had been on-course to drop out of hyperdrive behind the moon, but the huge ship's engines were running in response to non-suppressed impulses from its hyperdrive and had kept going too fast.

The navigator's hand struck the kill switch on the hyperdrive an instant before they would have struck Earth, but they were still just outside atmosphere. The ship was huge, and travelling fast. The navigator scrabbled to key in the emergency shuttle dump code, hoping to at least save the shuttle crews even if the main ship plummeted to the surface below. In his haste, though, he entered the wrong code, so that not just the occupied shuttles, but all the shuttles and escape pods dropped out of the ship. He could only hope that anyone in them would survive the crash. At least the emergency dump procedure prompted the shuttles and pods to automatically power up their shields. They would need it, hitting atmosphere at this speed; otherwise they would have been instantly killed by the atmospheric friction.

For another agonising millisecond, his hands flew, turning the ship's navigational controls around. Then he realised that he had done it. The great ship had spun around and its directional beam was pointing out into space again. He hit the hyperdrive button, but they were only metres from the planet's surface, in-atmosphere. It was a rough departure and he was relieved that by the time they re-entered hyperdrive they had come over an enormous ocean, where the probability of there being sentient beings within a few miles was much lower.

He had saved their ship, but they had lost all their shuttles and escape pods. Now they would have to go back to Earth to retrieve their people. His superior was not going to be happy.

But his captain's face was approving as he patted him on the shoulder, saying 'Well, done, navigator! That was close!'

'Sir, I ejected the shuttles before we struck Earth. We need to go back and retrieve our people.'

'Damn.'

'I'm sorry, Captain, I did not know whether we would hit the planet or manage to turn in time. It seemed appropriate to save as many lives as possible.'

'Yes of course, you did the right thing. But what caused us to overshoot? We need to know that before we go back in towards Earth. It could be dangerous.'

The navigator's hands flashed over his board, 'Sir, the hyperdrive seemed to maintain power for too long. When we came in close to the suppression field it should have died off, but the readings didn't change.' He looked up at his Captain with a worried expression, 'It's almost as though the suppression field had no effect, as though it were not working.'

'How many of our people are down there?' the Captain asked.

'We carry forty-two shuttles and one hundred and fifty-five escape pods, sir. Checking life-sign recordings now. We had twenty shuttles manned and sealed. The only pods that were manned were three that had maintenance crews in them. A total of two hundred and nine crew, sir.'

'That's not so bad.'

'Sir,' This was the part that the navigator did not want to tell his captain, 'We lost all the shuttles and pods, not just the manned ones.'

Only manned and sealed units should have ejected under evacuation procedures. 'What went wrong?' the Captain demanded.

'I hit the wrong code. I ejected everything.'

'But how the hell are we supposed to rescue our people if we don't have shuttles to send in after them?' The captain looked thoughtful, then the two looked at each other, 'The other battle cruisers!' the Captain exclaimed.

He looked at the navigator, who was nodding, 'Contact the nearest two ships and ask them to send shuttles down to the planet to retrieve our people.'

'Yes, sir.'


'I want to see the Geek, *now*!' Nick was huge, a tower of muscle, good looks and fighting ability and he was glaring at Ryan.

Ryan stared at the hulking footballer, who was swatting at

objects that floated in a little circle around his head.

'*Karl!* Get out here!' Nick yelled.

Karl Vendeman stepped out of his office, pushing his glasses back up on his nose. Nick sounded mad and Karl wondered what imagined slight he had inflicted on the hulking varsity player now. Then he stopped dead in his tracks when he saw the small metallic objects floating around Nick's head. Karl glanced back at Ryan, whose pen floated up to join the dancing objects floating around the very red-faced Nick.

Nick pointed up at his head, took a couple of deep breaths and growled, 'You did this. I don't know how, or why, but you did this to me.'

'What? What the hell makes you think it was me?' Karl asked.

'Because this is the sort of shit that you know about!' Nick roared.

'He's got a point,' Ryan agreed, earning him an incredulous look from Karl.

'Thanks for the support, Ryan!'

'So you did do it. Even he says so!' Nick said.

'That is not what he said, he said-' but Nick moved, picking up Karl by both shoulders and pinning him to the wall. Karl leaned back to duck the floating objects as they spun around Nick's head.

'Fix this up!' Nick said into his face. Karl could feel the heat of his angry face inches from his.

'I can't, I don't know-' Karl froze with fear as the huge ham fist curled up inches from his face.

Ryan objected. 'Hey, he didn't do anything,' but he was looking oddly at Karl.

'Well, who the hell else on campus could have done something like this?' Nick snarled and drew his fist back.

'You know, he has a point,' Ryan said, looking dubiously at Karl. 'Did you do something to him?'

'No, I didn't. God damn it!' Karl's temper flared and he yelled, 'Get your God-damned paws off me, Nick!'

Nick's curled hand froze and he stared stupidly at Karl.

'Well?' Karl's voice was tight, angry.

'I can't move,' Nick whimpered.

'What?' Karl asked and ducked out from between Nick and the wall.

'Let me go,' it was another whimper.

'Jesus, Karl,' Ryan wondered, getting scared, 'What can you do?'

'Nothing, nothing, I swear,' doubt crept into Karl's voice as he looked at the hulking footballer, frozen in a comedy of still rage with small objects still floating like Disney stars around his head, 'At least, I don't think I did anything to him.'

But then as Karl's attention was grabbed by a scream outside and he ran to the door out into the quadrangle. Nick slumped, released from the invisible force that had been holding him.

Ryan muttered to himself, 'The hell you didn't.'

Nick ran after Karl still bent on revenge and Ryan realized that people were screaming outside. He followed the other two boys out in to the quadrangle at a run. Students and lecturers were running out from their classes, then slowing and standing on the broad grass expanse, staring up at the sky.

Up in the plummeting shuttle above the campus, the pilot cursed them, and yelled at the view screen, 'Get back inside!'

It was hopeless, the shuttle was moving too fast and they were going to crash into the crowd of people which had started gathering on what had been a vacant expanse of lawn. He was close enough to see the white horrified faces looking up from the ground beneath him. Three young men, one of whom was grabbing the bigger one's shoulders, yelling and starting to run. But the bigger boy didn't run, just stared horrified at the shuttle and threw his hands up to stop it. The impossible, useless, gesture that all humans do by instinct, and the boy beside him did it too.

And suddenly without inertia, the shuttle stopped within a split second. The pilot and his crew should have been crushed with the force of it, should have been no more than bloody pulp against the inside of the viewing screen, but they floated, in the motionless shuttle a few feet from the three young men.

Nick was not the brightest boy on campus. He had got his placing there on a football scholarship. But he did have a very succinct turn of phrase, 'What the hell?'

He walked over to the metal shell of the craft and reached a hand up to touch it.

'I wouldn't do that, it may have shields,' Karl warned, but Nick touched it anyway and was unharmed.

He turned around and looked at Karl, 'Did we just stop this thing?'

'We?'

'Well, you both threw your hands up at it,' Ryan pointed out.

'No.' Karl whispered, then an idea occurred to him. 'Nick, stand back for a moment, will you?'

Nick stepped back and Karl squinted hard at the shuttle, which lowered a few inches. It stopped suddenly, then wobbled again, then smoothly lowered to rest on the ground.

'Jesus,' Nick said.

'Can you pick it up again?' Ryan asked Karl.

Karl said, 'I think so,' but he couldn't.

'You're not doin' it right,' said Nick and the sudden certainty in his voice gave Karl pause.

'What do you mean? How do you know what 'right' is?' Karl said.

'Yeah, who made you the guru?' Ryan asked sarcastically.

Nick shrugged, 'I mightn't know a lot about spaceships, but I do know you gotta put an effort in.'

Nick turned to the shuttle, he grunted and flung his hand in the air, and the ship lifted about three feet off the ground, then dropped like a stone and thumped back onto the turf, 'You were supposed to hold it up,' he accused Karl.

'Will you stop damned-well blaming me for everything that happens?' demanded Karl.

'Do you think there are aliens inside?' Nick was ignoring Karl and walking around the craft as he spoke.

'I don't know. I wonder if they're hostile? I wonder what they look like?' Ryan said, suddenly enthusiastic and curious.

'I wonder if they're hurt?' Nick said, earning him a speculative look from Karl. Nick had been the first of them to show compassion for the newcomers after the initial shock and fear. Perhaps there was more to this footballer than met the eye, after all.

'I never thought of that.'

'How do we tell? There doesn't seem to be a door or anything,' Ryan said, emerging from around at the back of the craft back to where they stood.

'There's a picture of one,' Nick observed, pointing to what looked like a painted-on doorway on the closest side of the craft.

Karl moved to the side of the craft, 'You know,' he said to Ryan, 'He's right, these lines could be the seams, it probably is a door. It's just that the seams are so fine we can't feel the join.'

'See, I'm not just a dumb hick footballer.'

Karl and Ryan both looked at Nick at the same time, then both decided they'd be silent rather than argue the point.

'Maybe,' Ryan suggested thoughtfully, 'Maybe you could open it like you stopped it, with your minds?'

'Let's try that,' Nick agreed.

Karl shrugged and stepped up beside Nick, 'So, what do you think….?'

'The hands thing seems to work,' Nick suggested, 'Let's give that a go.'

They raised their hands, made a few odd motions at the door and nothing happened.

Then a clear voice spoke in perfect English from inside the craft, 'Palm the lock, stupid!'

'Oh,' Karl said, feeling like an idiot and placed his hand over the hand-shaped image on the outside of the door. It opened so quickly that he didn't see the door slide back and all three boys jumped.

'Thanks,' mumbled the military looking type standing in the doorway. 'Captain Jean Poirot, Galactic Union Fleet Five, at your service, *sirs*,' and saluted Karl and Nick.

'Hey. Why are you saluting us?' Karl asked.

'Because you saved our lives. Thank you, *sirs*.'

'To hell with the sirs, thing, okay buddy? We're not military.' Karl said.

'Aye, *sirs*.'

Nick chuckled.

'Oh for Pete's sake, can you believe this guy?' Karl asked to no-one in particular, noticing that the crowd that had run out into the quadrangle to witness the crash, was now gathering around them.

'Hmm, maybe we should... Military Man, what was your name again?'

'Captain Jean Poirot, Galactic Union Fleet Five, at your service, sirs,' the alien responded. Nick was booming with laughter and Ryan was starting to chuckle.

'What?' Karl asked

.'I like this guy, he's funny,' Nick grinned, 'Can we have a look inside your space ship?'

'Sir, yes, sir.'

Down the road from the University, General Michael McCosker of the Alien Contact Intelligence Organisation of Earth sighed. It was so ironic. The Alien Contact Intelligence Organisation 'ACIO' was more than top secret. Only a handful of people had known about its existence until a few months earlier, until some internet nutcase troller had come across a careless website entry by a clerk who thought the organisation was a military retirement bureau.

Damn it, we're all old enough, thought McCosker, staring around his too-neat office. Most of the senior staff were just that, really senior. What's the good of having a top secret organization to deal with First Contact, when the damned aliens pull a stunt like this? Coming in, giving people super powers, arriving in a battle fleet. Lord's sake, where did that leave the ACIO? McCosker went over to the filing cabinet in the corner of his office, unlocked it, and pulled open the top drawer. He pulled out the largest object there, a rigid headband with two side arms which reached up over the ears and stopped in flat pads of electronics. He looked at the laser pointer next to it. Nothing unusual now in 2011, but back in 1947 it had them all floored.

'Sir!' his yeoman burst into the office without her usual polite knock.

'What is it, Harris?'

'Sir, there has been a landing, in the university quadrangle!' she said.

'Grab your jacket, we've all been flying desks for too long. Let's get out there amongst this!' McCosker strode out, tucking the headband and light pen under his arm and in his pocket. Maybe the damned aliens could at least tell him what it did.

'Yes, sir!' Harris was delighted and full of excitement, the way young people are when something out of the ordinary happens.

McCosker smiled. Harris's attitude reminded him what it was to be young. He cheered up as he followed the young woman out to his car. They headed down the road to the university campus and McCosker used his booming General's voice to say, 'Coming through, coming through, move aside please,' the crowd parted before them. They walked up to the shuttle. He stared at it entranced.

Several students were gathered outside the shuttle, and were they humans, emerging from the shuttle, in unfamiliar military style costumes?

McCosker stepped up and introduced himself, 'General Michael McCosker of the Alien Contact Intelligence Organisation. Who's in charge here?'

Ryan looked at him and pointed at Karl.

'Who are you?' McCosker demanded.

'Karl Vendeman, sir. We stopped this shuttle.'

'You what?'

'They saved us, sir,' spoke a tall, elegant man dressed in the strange uniform of the shuttle's occupants.

'Who are you?' McCosker said.

'Captain Jean Poirot, of the Galactic Union, sir,' Poirot said and snapped to attention with a salute. A tall hulking young student beside him giggled.

They all turned and looked at McCosker, whose mind was buzzing. Had the man said 'Galactic Union'? The implications of those two words swam in his head.

'My aide, Yeoman Genevieve Harris.'

Harris snapped an exemplary salute at Poirot, who stared at her puzzled, then saluted back much more casually than he had to the General. Nick raised an appreciative eyebrow at Harris and leaned over to whisper to her, 'Genevieve? Pretty name.'

She looked at him, craning her neck to do so and blushed. He grinned and turned away to the shuttle. 'Is everyone okay in here?' Nick called as he stepped with no particular caution into the craft.

He ducked as his head almost hit the top of the door and said, 'Hi,' to the nine crew members, two of whom were standing facing him with what looked like weapons, the other seven had now turned and were also facing Nick and the door. Nick took a quick look around and called back behind him. 'It's like a mini-bus, one that flies. There's two security guards and seven other peaceful-looking types. They look mostly human,'

Karl looked at Ryan, and Ryan said, 'Well, the technology is pretty advanced and this guy said 'Galactic Union', so maybe Nick was expecting a few aliens. You know, little green men, pointy ears,'

Karl shook his head and muttered, 'Hopeless, bloody hopeless,' and swung aboard the shuttle for a look.

Captain Jean Poirot stared about the quadrangle, then he, McCosker, Harris and Ryan followed Nick and Karl back aboard his shuttle. Poirot said curiously, 'This place looks peaceful.'

'Earth? It's pretty peaceful, most of the time. Why?' Karl asked.

'You are concerned with the welfare of my crew?' Captain Jean Poirot noted, becoming more and more curious. This was not what he had been led to believe Terran humans were like. Not only had they not shot the Galactic Union shuttle crew on sight, they seemed to be actively triaging them for injury and looking out for their welfare.

'Of course. That was a pretty rough landing,' Karl replied.

'It would have been rougher if you had not saved us,' Captain Poirot said, staring at his feet, looking ashamed, 'But, I suppose it doesn't matter anyway.'

Nick came back up to the front of the shuttle as he said that and the Captain's tone of voice and defeated look caught his attention, 'What do you mean?'

'I overheard our Fleet commander a moment ago on my communications unit saying that the suppression generator has failed and that we may need to destroy your planet, to get rid of all the violent life-forms there. It is likely that my crew and I will perish also.'

McCosker stared at him horrified, 'When is this supposed to happen?'

But Karl turned to Poirot and asked, 'Mind if we borrow your shuttle craft?'

McCosker looked at Karl, 'Why?'

Captain Jean Poirot stopped, then asked, 'What did you have in mind?'

'Well, to fly up and have a talk with your boss and persuade him that destroying Earth's surface would be a really bad idea?' Nick suggested.

Captain Poirot looked thoughtful and said, 'You promise not to hurt my people?'

'Are you for real? Okay, okay, we promise not to hurt them.' Nick said.

Captain Poirot looked around him, at the peaceful but now worried faces of the Terran humans and sighed, 'I have been lied to by the Union once too many times. I will help you, as you have saved us and only want to save your own people now.'

Karl looked into the back of the shuttle and asked 'Anyone need medical attention?' One of the Galactic Union soldiers nodded and closed his eyes looking a little shaken.

Nick said, 'I think this guy's a bit concussed.'

Karl said, 'Okay, get him out. Someone take him to the campus medical centre. The rest of you guys, you can stay on board, but we're taking your shuttle, okay?' The Union soldiers all looked to their leader for confirmation and Captain Poirot nodded, seeming strangely compliant to McCosker. The group of Terrans all gathered in the small space between the pilot's station and the bank of troop seats.

McCosker said, 'Come on. We don't know how long this Fleet commander of yours will wait before he sets his scorched Earth policy into motion.'

'Not very long, I am afraid,' Poirot said. He sat down and reached for the controls and they lifted vertically into the air. Poirot looked around at the Terrans behind him and said quietly, 'I did not touch the controls yet.'

'Just move,' McCosker said impatiently.

Poirot nodded and reached gingerly for the controls, then swung the small vessel around and took them back towards the upper atmosphere. The craft rose so swiftly and smoothly that the group behind him fell silent and Karl said quietly, 'Holy smokes,' as the sky darkened and three grey spaceships came into view. One was moving away from them, travelling back towards the other two.

The boys were silent and then Karl said, 'What the hell are we going to do? We can't fight them. They're massive.'

'Negotiate,' McCosker suggested grimly. He didn't like their chances of that, but it was their only option. He swapped a glance with Harris, whose eyes were like saucers. There was about a minute's silence as they approached the battle cruisers.

McCosker was holding something in his hands and Ryan heard a slight buzz from it and looked at it. Ryan said, 'What is that?'

'Oh, it's an alien artifact,' McCosker said. 'I don't know why I brought it.'

Captain Poirot picked up the artifact and tapped it. He shook it a few times, and a small blue light came on inside the upright wings of the headband. 'It's a mind shield,' he commented.

'A what?'

'A mind shield. It's like a personal protective device, stops psychic attack,' he looked thoughtful, 'It would have stopped the effects of that suppression field generator on your planet, too.

Where did you find it?'

'Archaeological diggings, out in the desert. We found this, too. What's a suppression field generator? You've mentioned that twice now.'

'Oh,' Poirot didn't look surprised, but McCosker noticed that he had not answered his question about the suppression field generator.

The General decided to get the information he wanted about the headband first. 'What is it, do you know? Looks like a light pen, to me.'

'Oh, sort of. It's a penknife, in your parlance,' Poirot said.

'How so?'

'Well, you can use it to recharge this, for a start,' Poirot twisted the pen and pointed it at the base of the headband, which lit up like a Christmas tree.

'Damn,' McCosker whispered.

'And, you can use it for all sorts of things, reheating coffee, cutting, laser pen,' Poirot fiddled with the pen and demonstrated as he spoke.

'What's a suppression field generator?' McCosker asked.

Poirot looked around at them all and sighed, 'You live on a prison planet. About twenty minutes ago the suppression generator which keeps it thus, was destroyed. That is why you Terrans are experiencing your natural psychic abilities for the first time.'

They all took that in and McCosker said 'So this generator that got blown up, it suppressed psychic abilities? Why would they need to do that? Humans aren't very psychic.'

'Aren't they just?' Poirot asked and pointed at Nick and Karl, 'These two stopped a shuttle in free-fall with just their minds.'

'They did that?' McCosker said.

'So it wasn't you?' Nick asked Karl.

'Wasn't me that what?' Karl asked.

'Made those things float around my head?' Nick realised.

'Oh no,' Karl said, 'You did that yourself.'

'But wait,' McCosker asked Poirot, 'What can humans do?'

'Not just any humans, Terran humans. From what I have seen, you are all inordinately powerful psychics. Perhaps from your powers being suppressed for so long. Of course, the more recent arrivals, like my father, would not have such abilities.'

McCosker realised why Poirot was willing to help the Terrans, 'Your father is down on Earth?'

'Yes. He was imprisoned there two years ago.'

'So that's why you were willing to help us,' McCosker relaxed. Up until now, he had been wary of Poirot and suspected a trap.

'So the headband,' Ryan asked, 'If I put it on, now, it would have no effect? Because the suppression generator is gone?'

'Yes,' nodded Poirot, raising an eyebrow at the quick intelligence of these Terrans, 'The generator has been destroyed. But the aliens who were stranded on Earth, must have had it so they could function even in the suppression generator's range. They must have known about the generator, so they were probably part of an authorised study team. However, if this was their only headband-' he stopped and looked enquiringly at McCosker.

'It was the only one we found, yes,' McCosker said.

'Well, they would have been stranded, then. It takes at least two minds to lift off a ship. Without a psi pair, you don't have the exponential power increase needed to achieve any useful level of psionic abilities. Three is better.'

McCosker was chewing his lip, looking worried. Harris noticed and sat down next to the old man, 'Problem, sir?'

'Well, lass yeah, I think we do have a problem,' McCosker said.

'What?' asked Harris.

'We only have one of these protection helmets, right?' McCosker's question was directed at Poirot.

'Well, yes, General.'

'And we're going to war with an enemy which has threatened to blow up Earth, and had the technology for this… psi suppression generator on the moon, thousands of years ago, right?'

'Yes,' Poirot sounded hesitant.

'Well son, if I were them, I'd be building more of those suppression generators, quick smart. So we need more of these,' the General said, 'and we need them yesterday.'

Poirot raised his eyebrows and pursed his lips. Harris nodded slowly in agreement. Ryan looked fascinated, 'So where do we get more of these?'

Poirot looked grim, 'They are manufactured near the Galactic Core, in a production facility there. It is the only one. The Union keeps its supply under strict control.'

They had everyone's attention now, even Nick and Karl's. The old General looked around at the young innocent faces around him and realised that amongst the lot of them, they didn't possess a bean of strategy. It made him nervous, but then he realised that for the first time in fifty-four years, he was useful. 'Son we need to beg, borrow, steal or manufacture more of these doo-hickies,' he said to Poirot, 'how would we go about that?'

'We can't steal them. The Galactic Core is too far away and we'd never get by their defences, without psi shielding. What are your people like at manufacturing?'

'Son,' McCosker smiled, 'You've come to the right planet. What do you need?'

'Gold. We need lots of gold.'

'Why?' Ryan asked.

'Because in here,' Poirot tapped the surface of the headband, 'is almost solid gold. The electronics focus it, channel it, make it a one-way street, but the gold is the basic damping material.'

'Wait,' Karl protested, 'Are you saying that gold suppresses psychic powers? And what do you mean, a one-way street?'

Poirot explained, 'Yes, of course gold suppresses psychic powers. That is why, when the Nuit visited your planet before the suppression field was in place, they gave your Egyptian leaders helmets of gold, to control them. That is why gold is so precious, to you it is precious because we have convinced you that it is. To us, it is precious because it protects us from you.'

'Shit,' Harris whispered, earning her a sharp glance from McCosker. She never swore.

'And what was that about the electronics and the one-way thing?' asked Karl.

'Oh, well, if you simply put a gold helmet on your head, it stops all psychic energy, incoming and outgoing. You are safe, but you cannot use your powers. The electronics is designed to set up a one-way field, that allows you to direct your power outwards, but does not allow energy to be used to attack or suppress you.'

'So it sort of polarizes the energy?' Karl asked.

'Well,'

'No son, it polarizes the damper field,' Mick McCosker said.

'Yes, that is a much more accurate description,' Poirot agreed.

'So these could come in handy?' Ryan said.

'Not just handy, son. I would say more they are a strategic imperative. We need to regroup and get a shipload of these little devices before we can defend Earth. Anything we tried without them, would be a suicide mission. You, Poirot, where's the best place around here to get the gold we need to the manufacture of these items?'

'Sir, our best option would be to return to Earth. There we can get gold and we can find workers who are not Empirical drones. Also, Earth's atmosphere is hospitable to humans, it will be easier to work there.'

'So, we need to stop these ships from destroying Earth, then get back to Earth and build a lot of these headbands?'

Poirot nodded, 'I wish you luck.'

'We'll need it.' McCosker looked grimly up towards the battleships ahead of them and said, 'Well, the suppression generator only got blown up about twenty minutes ago, you say? So, they won't have had time to build any portable suppression devices yet?' he looked to Poirot, who nodded. McCosker looked at the huge vessels, 'But in the meantime, how the hell are we going to commandeer those so that they don't blow us up?'

Nick was staring at one of the occupants of the shuttle seats behind them all, 'General, I think I know how we can do it.'

'How?' McCosker turned to him, then asked, 'What the hell is he doing?' The soldier in the seat was rubbing his stomach and patting his head.

'I'm making him do it,' Nick grinned.

'What, you mean we can control them?'

'I think we can control their minds, sir. When Poirot here started talking about psychic powers, I tried a bit of experimenting. It seems to work well.'

'Damn, well that should make it easier.'

'There are a lot of people on those battle cruisers,' Poirot warned.

'We'll just have to be careful and only take on small groups at a time. Can you tell me how to get on board and get to the main control room?' Nick asked.

Poirot sighed, 'Yes, I can.'

Nick grinned manically and Karl nudged him, 'Don't let the power go to your head, boy.'

'Why the hell not?' Nick grinned wickedly.

McCosker looked thoughtful, 'How far away do you think you can control someone's mind, Nick?'

'I don't know, sir. Why?'

'See if you can control the helmsman on that first big spaceship over there, son.'

'Control him to do what?'

'Just make the ship drift sideways a little, so we can tell if it's working.'

'Okay, I'll try,' Nick said. He closed his eyes and after a second, Karl groaned and held his head, 'Ouch.'

McCosker looked at them and then turned his attention to the ship ahead of them.

# CHAPTER SEVENTEEN

Back on Earth, three university students were leaning forward watching the television footage of the space ships on their widescreen, which was mounted high up on the wall.

One of them, a redhead, said, 'Oh man, this stuff's weird. I feel like I'm floating in the air.'

His female companion, Kim, giggled, 'You are floating, silly.'

Mikey looked down and laughed, 'Oh, yeah.'

'Hey Joe,' he called and the young woman screamed as Joe popped into existence beside them.

'Oh, way cool!' his friend said, 'How did you do that?'

'I dunno, I was in the kitchen and then you called me and I thought I should be here.'

They all laughed, then the girl said, 'Let me try,' and she blinked out of existence.

'Oh crap, what happened?' Joe asked.

'She'll be back,' his friend said. Indeed she was, blinking back into existence beside them, giggling uncontrollably.

'Where'd ya go?' Joe asked.

'The quadrangle,' she giggled, 'there are lots of people just floating up in the air. The lecturers are going nuts.'

'I'll bet,' Mikey said. He flicked out and appeared across the room, then said, 'Hey guys, we could go anywhere. Where do you wanna go?'

'Hey, I got a great idea,' Joe said looking back up at the television screen in the corner of the room, which was still showing an image of the two great spaceships, 'Let's go up and drive one of those ships around for a bit.'

'Sounds like fun,' grinned the girl and they all blinked out.

# CHAPTER EIGHTEEN

Zokar stared at the unconscious form on the bunk. She looked harmless enough, a bit too Fey-looking with her pale hair and eyes, a bit too human-looking with her full lips and round ears, but harmless enough. Appearances, he knew well, were often deceptive and here before him, lying unconscious on a bunk, lay one of the four most dangerous beings known in seven galaxies. Her powers, unleashed, could destroy worlds, could turn the minds of men in an instant to her cause and could stop a fleet in its tracks.

Zokar smiled, a simple sleeping draught, a whiff of gas, was all that it took to incapacitate her. She was, in this way, so human. He walked forward and lifted the pale face cautiously for a better look. She was almost nondescript, she was so innocuous looking. He sighed, committed her features to his memory for future reference and said to the guards, 'Get the medics to keep her well dosed up, we don't want her waking up. I'll be at the scanning station on the bridge.' He glanced across at Trudi, 'Keep them both drugged to the eyeballs.'

Zokar strode out, the two brig guards behind him and the senior brig guard went to alert the medics. The younger guard stepped forward cautiously, then mimicked Zokar's action in lifting Laura's pale face toward himself very gently. His heart was pounding because he knew that if she were awake or guarded he would be dead for this, but there was something compelling in the pale, modest face.

He heard the other guard returning and hastily resumed his post. The medics came in and set up sensor bracelets on Laura and Trudi which would automatically dose them with sedative if the concentration in their blood went too low.

Back on the bridge Zokar stared at the viewer showing what was happening on Earth.

'Sir.'

There was no response from Zokar.

'Sir,' Elesk, his cousin repeated, in a low but urgent tone.

'Mmmm?'

'We should go.'

'What?' he turned to look at her.

'We should go, sir. We have our prisoner.'

He frowned at her, not seeming to comprehend. 'The captain is not yet back on the ship.'

'With all due respect, sir, the captain is lost. He is planet side in a hostile environment with billions of newly psi-operant and violent Terran humans. He must be considered lost. Also, the Galactic Union is now aware of our presence here and is likely to send ships to investigate. We must leave this system.'

'No,' Zokar said and went back to his scanners.

She came around in front of him and grabbed his arm, 'We have the wealth, sir. We have the empress's daughter. We can turn and leave this mess behind.'

Zokar turned his silver eyes on his cousin and she shrank back at the look in them, 'Cousin,' he smiled sweetly, 'How would you like to be shoved out an airlock? Get back to your station.'

She stumbled backwards and ran back to her station. Zokar sat back from the scanners and considered his options. Elesk was correct. Of the four Galactic Union ships that had arrived near Earth, one had crashed on the planet below and another ship had narrowly missed crashing and was heading back to join the other two that were moving steadily closer to the Reingold. The logical thing to do would be to leave now.

He could not take on all three Galactic Union battleships. It was suicide. Zokar sighed, shook his head and cursed himself for a fool.

# CHAPTER NINETEEN

The three remaining Union Ships had regrouped and inched closer to the Reingold, which held its position. Zokar refused to budge and he sat in the central control room chair, tapping his foot with uncharacteristic impatience.

A Union shuttle had emerged from Earth's atmosphere and was heading towards the two Union ships. Zokar considered blasting it, but there was no need, the shuttle did not have sufficient weaponry to pose a threat to the Reingold and with any luck the Union ship that it was returning to might lower its shields to allow the shuttle back on board at some stage.

'Monitor their shields,' he reminded his crew, 'They might drop them to let that shuttle back on board.' Then Zokar fell silent and considered his options. They weren't good. The Reingold was outgunned by one of the Union ships, and they wouldn't survive a skirmish with three. Even if one of the Union ships did drop its shields briefly, if they attacked it then the other two ships would make space junk of the Reingold.

He could tell the Union ships that he had Laura on board and he would, as a last resort, if he thought they were going to attack. It was not his first choice, as he would lose the reward for returning her to the Galactic Core. However, it was the preferred option out of the two choices now open to him, being blown to pieces, or surrendering Laura. If he surrendered the empress's daughter back to the Union, at least the crew would survive and Zokar could rescue Shiva. He was going to hang onto Laura though, so that he had something to bargain with.

One of his weapons officers leaned forward toward his console.

'Spit it out man, what's happening?' Zokar snapped, on edge.

'Sir, one of the three Union ships appears to have started drifting,' the younger officer looked perplexed, 'It's drifting towards the other two ships; they will collide if they do not take evasive action,'

There was the flash of hyperdrive entry and one of the Union ships took off and sucked a vicious trail of hyperdrive wake right past the Reingold. It came so close that all the crew jumped, including the normally unflappable Zokar. Claxons sounded throughout the ship.

'What the galaxy?' Zokar said, then gathered his wits and yelled, 'Get a fix on that vessel, track them! They may be coming around for a flank attack!'

The helmsman studied his readouts intently, then announced, 'Sir, he went straight into maximum hyperdrive.'

Zokar stared at his helmsman. 'Straight into maximum hyperdrive? But that will take him halfway to the next star system. He won't be able to plot an accurate course back for weeks. What is he playing at?'

'Perhaps he is fleeing something, sir?'

Zokar slammed the communications unit on the command chair, 'Brig, are the two new prisoners still incarcerated?'

'Sir, yes sir, I am looking at them now. They are unconscious and safe.'

Zokar breathed a sigh of relief. He had thought for a second that Laura had woken up and managed to get herself aboard the Union ship without their knowledge, or that perhaps the Union ship had detected her life signs, sent a shuttle over under cloak and kidnapped her.

Zokar stared at the two remaining Galactic Union ships floating very still in space now, in front of the Reingold, with the shuttle edging closer and closer to them.

The Union Fleet Admiral chose that moment to contact the Reingold from the lead ship of the two remaining battle cruisers. He was not aware that the shuttle coming up from Earth was automatically picking up his signal and relaying it to every Earth channel it could contact as a result of the shuttle commander, Poirot, earlier trying to warn Earth defences of their impending crash. People hesitated in their daily activities as the Admiral's face appeared on their television channels.

The Union Fleet Admiral looked flustered, but determined. 'We have reason to believe you are harbouring a tribred aboard your vessel. Surrender this illegal creature to us or we will blow you into the next dimension. You are outgunned.'

So, thought Zokar, they have scanned us and discovered that we have Laura. It didn't help his strategic position.

On Earth, for the first time, Zokar Rizian's image appeared, his pale exotic face and glittering eyes implacable.

'Go to hell,' Zokar growled, his voice dropping an octave into a low and dangerous register.

The humans on the shuttle watched, amazed, as the aliens argued in English.

'I think all the Earth channels are getting this, too, General,' hazarded Nick, looking into the shuttle's communications screen, 'Actually, I think we might be re-transmitting it to Earth's satellite feeds. I'm not really sure how this system is rigged,' he admitted.

McCosker grinned and said, 'You're doin' just fine, son. And whoever that silver-eyed bastard is, I like him. He's got balls!'

The image switched back again to show the bland face of the Union's Fleet Admiral, who said in a threatening tone, 'We also intend to sterilize the surface of the planet below of all life forms. This is a standard operating procedure in cases such as this. I would advise you to surrender your prisoner and depart.'

All the humans on the shuttle blanched and McCosker jumped out of his chair, yelling, 'No!'

Cold silver eyes loomed large and dangerous in the view screen of the shuttle and most of the television news feeds on Earth. The alien said in an arctic tone, 'You do this, Admiral and the alliance between the Union and the Galactic Traders is over. You will need to go through my vessel first and the Reingold will not go down without a fight.'

Mick McCosker and his companions were horrified as they watched the scenes playing out before them on the view screen.

'We have to get aboard that battleship now and neutralise their weapons!' McCosker exclaimed.

'How?' Karl asked.

'Like this!' Nick said and grabbed the controls from Ryan and drove hard at the shuttle entry bay of the nearest Union battleship, stretching his mind out to find the minds of the people within 'Get us through safely!' he yelled at Karl, who stared at the closed bay doors rushing up to meet them.

Nick reached out a beefy hand and grabbed Karl's hand, 'Like this!' he repeated and suddenly Karl understood and tried to reach the minds of the people controlling the shields and the shuttle bay doors. At the last minute, he and Nick succeeded and the shields dropped and the bay doors opened, allowing the shuttle access. 'Knock them out,' ordered McCosker to Nick, who looked at the Union shuttle crew, and they all slumped, unconscious.

'Ow,' Karl complained, holding his head.

'Sorry buddy, no time to waste, they're threatening Earth,' Nick patted Karl on the shoulder.

'What the hell, are you using my mind somehow?'

'It would appear so,' McCosker said. 'Whatever happens on board this ship, I want you two,' he pointed at Nick and Karl, 'to stay together and stay with me.' They stepped out into the oxygen rich atmosphere of the ship's shuttle bay.

'Let's find the control room on this monster,' McCosker suggested and they followed him towards the internal bay doors into the ship.

Back on board the Reingold, Zokar was distracted by more strange reports from Weapons and Helm, 'Sir, we are getting some very odd readings on the two Union ships,' the young weapons officer looked incredulous, because before him on the schematic of the Union ship, a row of dots around the edge of the ship was fading out, one by one, 'Sir, the ship the shuttle docked into has not put its shields back up! And the lead ship is dropping its shields too!'

'Have they gone mad? In the middle of hostile territory and a confrontation, they are dropping their shields? In Earth orbit???' Zokar said.

'Sir, the other ship appears to be drifting, too… wait, no, they appear to have some helm control now.'

'It's a trick, it has to be.'

'Should we fire on them?'

Zokar hesitated, uncharacteristically. Normally he would have fired, but what if Shiva had managed to commandeer that shuttle?

'No. Wait.'

His crew looked at him puzzled, but waited. The weapons officer had his hand over the firing button and was watching Zokar's face intensely. Long minutes passed and nothing changed.

'Incoming communication, sir.'

'Put it on the screen, Helmsman,' Zokar replied, his voice curious but still calm.

The view screen flashed several times, then there was static and the screen cleared, to reveal an odd group of humans in strange clothing gathered in the control room of the Galactic Union ship and the Union crew standing around looking like zombies, their hands and eyes drifting to and from communications controls as several of the younger humans stared intently at them.

'This is General Mike McCosker of the planet Earth, come in alien vessel, do you read me? Please do not fire upon Earth or this vessel, we mean you no harm. Do you read me?' The General's voice was urgent and sounded worried.

'Zokar Rizian here, General Mikemickosster,' Zokar said, 'Are you receiving me? Am I correct in assuming that you have just commandeered that Union battle cruiser?'

'Yes! We had no choice, you heard. They threatened to destroy Earth! Did you just save our planet by stopping those bastards?'

'Well yes.' Zokar decided that it was best to have the Terran humans on side, so he did not point out that his only real interest was rescuing the Reingold's captain. Perhaps he could even gain their assistance in finding Shiva?

'Hot damn, Mr Soccer Risen! You are now officially a bona-fide Galactic Hero! What can we do to help you?'

Zokar sat back in his chair and smiled.

'Do you have control of that ship next to you?'

'No.'

'Then let a shuttle from my ship come and get some of your party and we will go over there and get control.'

'Oh, I think we can do that from here, sir, we are getting better at this as we go. Thrown in the deep end and all that.' McCosker turned to Ryan, 'Take Harris and concentrate on controlling those officers over on that other ship, Ryan. Let me know if you haven't managed it within one minute and I'll get Nick and Karl to help you.'

'Sir, yes sir!' Harris snapped to attention. Ryan groaned.

'Mr Risen? Do you read?'

Zokar smiled again, 'Yes, General Mikemickosster?'

'I assume that those fellows over in that other ship will not fire on this vessel, because their buddies are all over here still. Do you concur?'

'It would seem unlikely that they will fire upon you,' Zokar agreed.

'You sir, and your ship have no such protection. I suggest you move around so that this vessel is between you and them,' McCosker said.

'Helm, comply,' Zokar ordered, nodding. Damn, these humans did tactics like second nature.

The young helmsman moved the Reingold carefully so that the remaining Union vessel could not fire upon them without hitting the ship McCosker's crew was on.

Zokar was thoughtful. He knew that the complement on the Union battleships was over 1200 crew. If McCosker and his small bunch of humans were to keep control of them, they would probably be stretched.

'General, do you have any objections to my sending over a support crew for you? You are going to need interpreters and bridge crew that can operate without you controlling them, or you will all collapse with exhaustion in a few more hours. We can send security over, to organise the Union prisoners. Do you agree to this?'

'That sounds alright, sir. My men on the shuttle have been busy, they report that they had mesmerised the crew of the other vessel before we got up here. Perhaps you could send a crew over there too?'

'So, that is why the Union Fleet Commander did not fire on either of our vessels. Of course I will send a crew. Stand by to receive shuttles.'

'Oh, and Soccer Risen?'

'Yes, General?'

'I think you will find that your profile on Earth is pretty positive. Our shuttle communications found their way via satellite feed to Earth. You're all over the news. Karl, show him the feed if you can, replay it for him.'

Karl waved a hand at the communications officer on the Union ship and suddenly a news feed from Earth occupied the view screen before Zokar. It showed the scene minutes before, with Zokar's ice-cold voice dominating the air waves, 'Go to hell,' Zokar saw himself say, in a low, menacing growl.

The screen cut to a shot of the impassive Union Fleet Commander, 'We also intend to sterilize the surface of the planet below of all life forms. This is a standard operating procedure in cases such as this. I would advise you to surrender your prisoner, and depart.'

Zokar watched his own face with a detached interest, had he really looked that angry? He looked ready to chew up the hyperdrive core on the Union ship, 'You do this, Admiral, and the alliance between the Union and the Galactic Traders is over. You will need to go through my vessel first and the Reingold will not go down without a fight.'

The feed cut back to an over-excited Earth journalist, saying, 'And that, people, is our first contact with the alien called, Soccer Rizian. Thank you for saving our planet. The military assures us that they now have the situation under complete control and that an alliance is being sorted out as we speak. But today, ladies and gentlemen, this man is the hero of the hour.' It cut back to a picture of Zokar, who, as he watched the feed replay, had to exert all his self-control to maintain military decorum and avoid squirming with embarrassment in his seat.

'Thank you, General. It is most enlightening.'

'Thank you, sir.'

Zokar thought for a moment, then leaned forward in his seat, 'General, if I may ask a favour?'

'Well yes, I certainly think so,' McCosker smiled.

'Sir, I have a friend, lost on the surface below. I wonder if your people might help me to find him?'

'Sure thing, Soccer, sure thing!'

Zokar flinched again at the Terran pronunciation of his name, but sighed in resignation. He had the humans of Earth on side, as a group.

# CHAPTER TWENTY

A change was happening on Earth. The Earth collective mind had sensed a threat to the blue planet and the native life forms on it. The response was less like a whisper, and more like the thunderous roar of a crowd.

Normally the Terran mind did several things when it spoke, part of the process being to translate tenuous thoughts into words. Thoughts were most easily read when they were formed as speech but were not yet spoken. Any earlier in the process and the receiving telepath received nothing but vague impressions, which they then had to put into words themselves. These words often differed from the words the other person involved in the telepathic communication would have produced from the same thoughts. But in this case no such problems were encountered. It was as though hundreds and even thousands of minds became as one person, thinking and feeling the same things.

The suppression generator was gone, and every creature on the planet Earth had been threatened. Every newly operant human, every newly operant animal and plant. They all knew about the generator, they all knew about the Union Fleet Commander's threat to destroy the surface of Earth, and they all knew everything that was going on in the hearts and minds of all those around them. Individual minds moved to protect themselves, shutting out huge volumes of information they couldn't cope with at the time, but all they had to do was wonder and relevant knowledge would flood into their minds at will.

The Union was soon to find out why this planet was called the 'Deadly Jewel.' That name had come down though the millennia. It had first been used when an angry mining magnate running the gold mines of Egypt, controlling the pharaohs with the clumsy gold helmets, had screamed in rage one day and threatened the Terrans with laying waste to their planet if they did not cooperate with his plans.

The Terran group mind had banded together then, even though

the Terran humans could not help much. The humans had been hampered by the golden torcs and the golden helmets which they thought of as signs of status. Little did they know that the gold in those prized artifacts was suppressing the psychic abilities of all the humans, especially the powerful pharaohs. But although the Terran humans were hampered, there were other native creatures on Earth besides humans.

Back then, the entire Terran ecosystem had risen up against the alien Egyptian mining magnates. Locusts swarmed the crops of the Egyptians, so that the aliens had no food for the long journey home and could not escape Earth. Lions and jackals stalked the palace walls at night, hunting aliens. Mosquitos and rats bit and infested the aliens. In desperation, blaming the pharaohs, suspecting subterfuge, the aliens killed and buried the pharaohs in their restrictive gold helmets and entombed the most powerful of them in massive pyramids of stone. Traps of poisonous gases were left to be tripped if anything stirred in the sarcophagus rooms, for it was known even back then that an unconscious Terran human could not use their mental powers. But despite all their efforts the aliens were massacred, spurring the Galactic Union to install the suppression generator to prevent a recurrence.

But now the suppression generator had been destroyed and the modern Terrans knew everything that McCosker knew about the mind-shields, they knew everything they needed to know about making them and without a word, they began to work together to preserve their planet, to ensure their survival. They accessed the mind of an unfortunate technician on one of the Union ships who knew the physics behind the suppression generator and shields and that particular tech slumped to the floor as his mind was drained of that knowledge.

Now, as in the time of the pharaohs, the Terran humans, plants and animals helped each other out without question, without predation, with a sudden willing suspension of the rules of eat-or-be-eaten, in favour of the new and temporary rule of 'unite and survive.'

A lion in Africa stopped its headlong charge towards the baby elephant it was closing in on.

A cobra lowered its hood and the mongoose and the cobra turned their eyes skywards, sitting side-by-side, their attention fixed on what they saw in their minds. The mongoose stood and started to walk away, with the cobra slithering beside it.

The weapons stilled, and the shooting stopped in Pakistan, Libya and Afghanistan.

The number of hits on Google dropped to zero and stayed there.

McCosker felt it and stilled, put his hand out and asked, 'What the hell is that?' to anyone listening and no-one in particular.

The non-Terran humans on the Union ship felt ill and unable to move. The Terrans who had invaded them felt a spring in their step, as though the energy of a dozen people had been placed at their disposal.

# CHAPTER TWENTY-ONE

Zokar paced from scanning station to scanning station on the bridge of the Reingold. His bridge crew was nervous and the silver-haired elf was irritable beyond belief.

'Haven't you found anything yet?' he demanded of Elesk. She shook her head miserably and started to speak, 'Sir-' but saw the look on his face and hesitated.

'What?' he demanded.

'Well, sir, Captain Kiran is human sir, pure blooded human.'

'Your point being?' Zokar knew Shiva was a pure blooded human. It was one of the things in which his friend took an illogical pride, almost as if he had control over his genetics at birth. Then again, Zokar had to admit the occasional sense of satisfaction in his own mind about being a purebred old Elvish being, so who was he to criticise Shiva?

'Sir, with all due respect, we are searching a planet full of some of the most pure bloodlines of humans in the galaxy. On a planet of seven billion purebred humans, we are seeking one purebred human.'

Zokar scowled at her, 'Stop making excuses and scan!' he snapped.

Elesk sighed and returned to her scanning, wondering for all the worlds what good it would do her. Then again, better to look at the scanners than risk Zokar blowing her head off, she had never seen him in a worse mood.

A beep from the central chair distracted Zokar, 'Reingold, Rizian,' he snapped into the comm.

'Zokar, my lad, it's Mick McCosker. Any luck finding that friend of yours yet?'

'No, but thank you for asking.'

'Hey, I won't beat about the bush. I need a favour. We need some more crew members up on these ships and I was wondering if you could send a shuttle or two down to pick up another fifty men? I'd be much happier if the ships were fully manned with friendlies before our skeleton crew up there starts to drop off to sleep.'

'Of course, General, it would be my pleasure. Send the coordinates through and we will have a shuttle there in fifteen minutes. Oh, and General?'

'Yes, Zokar?'

'Do you have any suggestions for expediting our hunt for the captain? We are having difficulties because he is of pure human blood and therefore indistinguishable from the rest of your populace.'

'Well, you could go back to basics '

'What do you mean, sir?'

'You know where he was dropped off right, what coordinates?'

'Yes.'

'Well, he can't have moved far from there. You could instigate a search for him within a ten mile radius of that point. Or we could, if you have a photo of him somewhere, a good portrait, head and shoulders say?'

'I do have one like that. I will send an image down shortly. General, I thank you.'

'You are most welcome, Zokar my boy. Good luck finding him and thanks for the shuttle.'

'Good evening, sir.'

Zokar cut off the communications link and stood up, 'I'll be in my quarters. I will be back shortly.'

He strode through the ship and eventually came to his quarters. The door scanned his appearance, body parameters, retinal pattern and and quickly correlated all that with his recent shipboard activities. His computer use log showed that his recent activity on the bridge had ceased several minutes earlier and his physical appearance matched that on record. All this was correlated within a second, after which the door flicked open to admit Zokar.

Zokar strode into the familiar icy cold room and walked up to the wall over his bed, where there was a recent photo of him and Shiva on shore leave at one of the ocean planet resorts near the Galactic Core. The photo was clear and showed the human's characteristic smile and tanned, open face. Zokar reached up and keyed the code on the frame that would send a copy to the bridge, then stopped for a moment to look at the photo under his hands. His harsh elvish face softened and he smiled, he remembered the day clearly, Shiva had been horrified to discover that elves not only can swim like fish, but that elves love to eat raw fish whole.

Zokar, on his part, was amazed that humans didn't eat raw fish. He watched Shiva butcher and burn a perfectly good meal of baroola fish until it was too soft to get his teeth into, then ruin it further by adding salt and juice from a sour citric fruit. Zokar had laid back watching Shiva, contented, with his belly swollen with freshly killed and eaten fish, and wondered not for the first time about the nature of humans.

The elf shook himself from his unnecessary reverie and left his cabin to go and supervise the scanning activities of the crew on the bridge of the Reingold.

Soon, the image of General McCosker filled the screen of the Reingold. Back on the bridge, Zokar Rizian was discussing their options for defending Earth with the General.

'Where did that third ship go?' Zokar Rizian said, pacing up and down the bridge.

'We don't know for sure,' McCosker admitted. He, too, paced up and down, but on the bridge of the Union battle cruiser which he had commandeered, 'It went into hyperdrive in the direction of the Core, but that could have been just the way it was aiming at the time. It was returning to the other two ships at the time and they were on a vector coming out from the Core.'

'Damn,' Zokar said.

'You anticipating trouble?' McCosker asked.

Zokar gave him a long look, 'Terran, do you know what you are setting yourself up against?'

'No. I'm guessing by the size of these cruisers, though, it ain't a penny ante operation.'

Zokar recited what every four year old should know, 'The Galactic Union encompasses seven galactic civilisations, and comprises forty-nine member sectors. It is ruled by the family of Keallach, which has ruled it for seventeen millennia.'

McCosker screwed up his face.

Nick came up beside McCosker and gazed intently at Zokar through the view screen.

'Yes?' Zokar asked, looking at the handsome young man with a sense of trepidation.

'You knew that, and you stood up against them? Why?'

'I told you, to protect the Earth.'

'No, I could understand that coming from a human, but what's Earth to you?'

Zokar was tight-lipped.

Nick looked at him with sudden insight, 'This captain of yours who is lost down here, you would take on this Galactic Union that you just described, for him?'

Zokar cut him off with a scathing rebuke, 'What I do and who I do it for are none of your business, stranger.'

McCosker and Nick exchanged glances and grinned. There are some things that military men and footballers understand and appreciate intuitively, and one of those things is loyalty.

McCosker said, 'Zokar, meet Nick. Nick, Zokar.'

The two nodded at each other stiffly.

Behind Zokar, Nick saw Elesk smiling.

'Well, son, believe it or not we do understand where you are coming from,' McCosker smiled.

Zokar stared at them. He was at least nine hundred years older than McCosker, and the General had just called him 'son.'

'So,' McCosker said, 'What is this Galactic Union likely to do next?'

'Damage control,' Zokar said grimly, 'General, I hate to say this, but your planet is in a bit of bother.'

'Tell me all about it, son. In fact why don't you bring a shuttle over here and we can have dinner together and talk about it?'

'Thank you, but I have important cargo on board, that I am loath to leave, General. Why don't you bring a couple of your associates and we'll talk about it on board the Reingold. The food here is much better, too. Oh, and Nick?'

'Yes, Zokar?'

'You are included in the invitation.'

'Thanks,' Nick smiled.

Zokar sent Elesk down to Earth for a few hours to help with the search for Shiva. He would have gone himself, longed to go himself, but he knew that if he left the ship there was every chance that Elesk would simply take Laura back to the Core to collect the reward without him or Shiva. Zokar knew she would come back for them, but he was not willing to take the chance that before she got back, the Galactic Union would find out what was happening out here and attack Earth again. This time with a much bigger force.

Zokar needed his ship and he needed the alliance with the Terran humans and their unique abilities to defend Earth until he found Shiva. He could do with Laura conscious and cooperative, but he did not know how he could achieve that, so chose to leave her unconscious and out of the equation for now. He knew he could not do that indefinitely, but he did not want to wake her up and find out she was on the side of the Union, or worse, the Fey. He considered the human she had with her. Perhaps he could wake that one up and see if she could provide more information on which way the empress's daughter would be inclined to jump.

He was tossing up his options, when the helmsman in front of him stiffened and reported, 'Fifteen more Galactic Union battle cruisers have just come into scanner range, from outside the Solar system, sir. On course to Earth and moving fast.'

Zokar swore, 'Shields up, monitor them. Warn McCosker's vessels. We are going to need more help than McCosker can give with this one. Helmsman, take the con, I will be in the brig.'

He strode off the bridge. He calculated they only had about fifteen minutes before those vessels were within firing range. Fifteen minutes in which to convince the woman he had kidnapped and drugged that they should work together.

Zokar arrived at the brig and said to the guards, 'Release the force field. Reverse their drug regime. I want them lucid in two minutes.'

The medical technician nodded and dialled something on the bracelets around Laura's and Trudi's wrists. Zokar stood waiting as the young women stirred, groaning, from their drugged state.

'Oh jeez, my head,' Laura groaned and sat up.

Beside her, the dark haired one asked, 'What happened?' Then they both looked at Zokar and froze.

Zokar said quietly and quickly, 'We need your help. The Galactic Union is trying to render Earth uninhabitable and this ship of ours is the only thing standing in its way.'

'Uninhabitable how?' the dark haired one asked. Laura was staring at him appraisingly.

'The standard method is to use a barrage of disruptor fire which destroys all life forms instantly,' Zokar said.

Laura asked him, 'You need our help? It sounds more to me like we need your help. Why are you so worried about what happens to Earth?'

'My captain and a large contingent of my crew are down on your planet's surface. Without your help, they will be destroyed along with the rest of the inhabitants of Earth. We both therefore have a common interest in preventing this from happening. Will you help me?'

'Why did you drug us then?' Trudi asked, rubbing her eyes, 'Why didn't you ask for our help straight away?'

'Laura is a valuable hostage. My captain's intention and mine was to return you to your family at the Galactic Core and collect a reward for your return.'

'My family is on Earth. What are you talking about?' Laura said.

'Ah, Laura,' Trudi said guiltily, 'That's not quite true.'

Laura stared at her and Trudi nodded, 'I'm sorry, but it's quite possible that he's telling the truth.'

'What are you saying, Tru? How do you know this?'

'I was five when they brought you to live with us, Lor.'

Laura stared at her blinking, as Trudi turned to Zokar and asked gently, 'Couldn't you have just gone anyway without your captain? Why did you bother waking us up? Why not just turn and run?'

Zokar lifted his head and gave her an unreadable look, but did not reply. Laura was still blinking stupidly at Trudi, then abruptly she shook herself and asked Zokar, 'What do you need us to do?'

Zokar nodded gratefully and said 'Come with me, I will show you.'

'So you're not really my sister?' Laura asked Trudi, a little indignantly, as they left the brig.

# CHAPTER TWENTY-TWO

The fleet of fifteen Galactic Union ships had dropped out of hyperdrive and was threatening the Reingold. Zokar Rizian knew they were in serious trouble, as Laura was still dopey from the strong drugs he had used to put her under and did not have a clear idea of how to use her powers. He had three ships against fifteen and the Reingold, for all its arsenal of weapons was at heart a giant transport, not a battleship. Much as he loved the Reingold, Zokar knew his vessel's limitations and he knew that the current situation well exceeded those limitations. For a start, the Reingold did not have the manoeuverability of the Galactic Union Battle Cruisers they were facing.

The Galactic Union Admiral on the nearest battle cruiser to the Reingold snapped at his aide, 'Put this on all channels. I want the Earth people on the planet to hear it too!'

'Aye, sir.'

The Admiral waited for the tell-tale lights to come up, indicating the channels he had requested were all open, then snarled, 'People of Earth, this is Admiral Kamodo of the Galactic Union. You will cease your hostilities or we will destroy your planet.'

Down on Earth, people stilled and watched their view screens. Sudden anger washed through the Terrans, from man, woman and child, like a tsunami. Something changed in the air and the people watching the transmission felt it. They looked at each other in wonder as their minds began to link together, like Roman soldiers grouping into a phalanx and raising their shields. The natural mental state of Terrans when threatened, is to unite. It was unfortunate for the Galactic Union that they did not realise that until too late.

McCosker's men on the second Galactic Union Battle Cruiser that had been commandeered had figured out how to use the weapons system and began firing on the Admiral's fleet, with deadly accuracy. Three ships were destroyed within the first minute.

On the Admiral's ship, the communications unit showed the disastrous results of his threat, including the destruction of the Union ships. They showed the angry faces of the Terran crew looking up at the view screens, the expressions on their faces strangely identical, strange slim headpieces over their ears.

The Admiral's aide commented wryly, 'Well, that worked well, didn't it?'

'Sir, we have an incoming transmission.'

'Put it on screen,' the Admiral sighed.

Zokar Rizian's face appeared, looking cold and furious, 'Admiral, the planet Earth has made no hostile overtures towards the Galactic Union. What excuse do you offer for making this threat to attack a defenceless and densely populated planet?'

'You have our leader.'

'If you want her, come and get her,' Zokar smiled and the Reingold powered up and moved away.

'What are you doing?' Laura asked.

'Trying to get them away from your planet,' Zokar said, 'Weapons, send a couple of shots across their bows. Draw them out.'

'Follow that ship!' the Admiral said, 'Track him! If he goes into hyperdrive, I want to know what heading he was on when it happened!'

'They're firing, sir. Shall we return fire?'

The Admiral's face was grim, 'Yes. They have fired on us. They have initiated hostilities. Never mind the hostage, we have no choice but to defend ourselves now.'

The battle cruiser sent a barrage of fire towards the Reingold and the Reingold spun slowly around to fight. But before the giant Reingold had completed its turn, it was hit badly, two strikes amidships, one too close to the bridge for comfort. Zokar was looking into the scanners on the captain's console to check damage to the Reingold, but suddenly jumped up with a shout of warning and threw himself in front of Trudi and Laura on the bridge, as a segment of the bulkhead above the two women collapsed.

Laura said, 'Thanks,' as they pushed the bulkhead aside and she stood up, but then she saw the silver blood coming from the elf's side.

'You're hurt!' Laura exclaimed.

'It would appear so,' Zokar replied, struggling against the dead weight that was his legs, trying to stand up.

Laura turned to Trudi and blanched. Trudi's eyes were closed, and she was still slumped on the floor, 'Trudi! What's wrong with her, Zokar?'

He looked over at the dark-haired human woman, 'She's still breathing. She must have been knocked out. Here, lie her out properly so she can come to when she's ready.'

'We should get the medics!' Laura said.

'The medical bay was destroyed by that first shot. I'll have a look at her when I'm up in a few moments.'

Laura nodded. She didn't know whether Zokar was in much better shape than Trudi. She turned back to face the view screen, even though she knew the battle was lost before it began. Even with the destruction of three of the fifteen Union ships, that still left twelve vessels against their three. The Terrans on board the Reingold and the commandeered battle cruisers, even with all their abilities, were simply too inexperienced in this form of battle. They were too slow on the manoeuvres, too slow to evaluate tactics, hell, *she* was too slow. Even Zokar Rizian had admitted that they were outgunned. That last ship should not have got past her awareness, her shields.

Laura held her head and felt sticky blood over the pain, felt her awareness dulled. She stared down the barrels of the Union battleship and gritted her teeth, waiting, counting her last seconds. Zokar managed to stand up beside her, his elvish face pained, he was bleeding silver blood from a wound in his side and his face was pale. He reached out to steady himself and found Laura's arm, but she was sagging, too.

'Damn them,' Zokar whispered, glancing groggily at Laura's face, his eyes confused.

Laura looked at him, but she was taking deep breaths and kept looking off to the right of the view screen, screwing her face up in concentration.

'What?' Zokar gasped, following her gaze.

'Zokar,' she gasped, 'Something's coming.'

He indicated with a weak six-fingered hand, the ship before them, and pointed back at himself and Laura, 'Yes, about a trillion megawatts of energy in the form of their main guns.'

He sank to his knees, gritting his teeth, shaking his head to clear it, fighting the oncoming darkness. Elves do not die easily.

'No,' Laura said, gripping his arm tighter and pointing with her other hand to the upper right of the view screen, 'From up there.'

'Wha...?' but Zokar sagged down beside her in a crumpled heap and passed out next to Trudi.

The Union battleship before them erupted in a massive explosion which blossomed out in a neat circle. She stared, then screamed, 'Evasive!' and saw the young helm officer, arm sliced in three places, bleeding, trying to comply. Laura lurched forward, trying to help, but a wave of dizziness stopped her and she stared, confused, at another Union battleship emerging from the top right of the view screen. Then the communications unit beeped, and the screen changed, and a jet-haired man appeared on the view screen and time slowed down for Laura. The man turned and looked into her eyes, everything slowed down around them both. Voices stilled, explosions froze in mid-expansion and the universe ground to a strange, chilly halt.

Laura said, quietly, into the sudden silence around her, 'Hello.'

'Hey. Are you alright?'

'I am now. Thanks to you?' She glanced around her, but knew that she had done this and he had. It was as it should be. There was no threat from this familiar face before her.

He watched her for a moment, then smiled and confirmed, 'Yes, thanks to me. I am glad I arrived in time.' He stopped and seemed to be waiting for something from her, then asked, 'Do you know who I am?'

She looked at him, then looked around her, 'No,' She looked perplexed. Was this a dream? It could be, with the strange distortion of time.

He smiled.

She added, 'You saved me. Why? Who are you? Why aren't you on their side?'

'Of course I saved you,' he laughed.

Laura asked, 'Who are you?'

He looked at her and she looked into his black eyes. Looked into eyes that sparkled with joy and sudden realisation dawned.

'Are we related?'

He smiled and said simply, 'I am your twin brother, Dom. I have spent twenty-two years looking for you.'

She stared at the view screen, dumbfounded.

# CHAPTER TWENTY-THREE

'Dom' she tried the name in her head and spoke it, 'I do not recognise your name.'

'You wouldn't. You were stolen as an infant. What do they call you?'

'Laura. They call me Laura. But, how do I know that I can trust you. That you are who you say you are?'

'Laura,' he said, testing the alien-sounding syllables on his tongue. Then he remembered that she had asked an important question, 'Could anyone else do this?' he raised his hands at the frozen world around them.

'What have we done?'

'It's called stasis. Stopping time or slowing it down. Only you or I can do it throughout such a large volume of space. Only we together can hold it at will, or reverse it.'

'Reverse it?'

'Yes. Others can perform simple acts of slowing time down, but only we together can stop time on such a large scale and reverse it at will.'

You and I together? You say we are twins, does this have something to do with it?'

'Have you heard of psychic pairs?'

'Yes well, sort of. I know what you mean. Two people who when they work together have exponentially greater psychic powers than they do as individuals. Like Nick and Karl.'

'I do not know those names, but it sounds like you have the right idea. Put succinctly, our family are extremely powerful psychics, which is why we rule the Union. When twins are born into the family, which is rare, those twins form a very powerful psychic pair, which makes ruling the Galactic Union easier for them and brings peace to the Galaxies.'

She was silent, considering all this. Then she looked up and said, 'So you are on the Union's side?'

He laughed, 'So are you. We two together, are the Galactic Union.'

'Dom, you have seen, what is happening around us, right? Your Union attacked my planet.'

'Your planet? This is a prison planet, to which you were illegally taken. That does not make it your planet. Well, technically, I suppose it makes it one of billions of your planets…'

She was already shaking her head, 'You don't understand.'

'Of course I do. Don't be insulting,' he bridled.

'I'm not. You do not understand Earth.'

'What do you mean? What do I not understand about Earth?'

'These psychic pairs that you were talking about?'

'Yes.'

'What if an entire planet could form a psychic union?'

Dom went pale, 'That, you are talking about billions of souls. Trillions of souls, if you count all the life forms,'

'Yes.'

'What planet has done this?'

She looked pointedly at Earth.

'No,' gasped Dom, 'Not the Terrans. No,' he shook his head in horror.

'Yes, the Terrans. And mostly thanks to you guys.'

'What? Why?'

'Your Admirals, in all their wisdom, threatened Earth.'

'So?'

'They threatened to destroy Earth.'

'Oh,'

'Yes, 'oh'. The native creatures that populate this planet, however aggressive and predatory towards each other in normal times, when facing an outside threat develop an instant psychic network to protect the ecosystem. The humans you banned to this planet absorbed this psychic tendency, but it lay dormant. But after the suppression generator was destroyed and your people threatened Earth, the humans were included in the psychic network formed by the creatures of Earth to protect themselves. You have caused the birth of a psychic power in the Galaxy that makes your abilities and mine, insignificant by comparison. There is one further complication.'

'What?' Dom whispered, wondering how what she had described could possibly get worse.

'When the Terran group mind network was activated, I was included in that activation.'

'Oh, shit,'

'So, my new brother, now do you understand when I say Earth is my planet?'

Dom looked horrified, 'But you need to come back to the Galactic Core, with me. The Union is tearing itself apart with warring factions as we speak! I cannot leave you here to guard this insignificant little planet!'

'You're losing me,' she warned.

'I demand that you return with me! I have spent twenty-two years looking for you! Doesn't that count for anything?'

'And they,' she said, looking back at Earth again, 'Have spent twenty-two years caring for me. Would you have me leave them to their destruction?'

'No, but you say that the Terrans are powerful in their own right, surely they can protect themselves now without you?'

'And why should they have to do without me? So that your conglomerate of alien races can flourish? I'm sorry, the Terran humans are getting off to a shaky start. My presence here will ensure their survival.'

'And your presence is needed with me at the Core to ensure the Galactic Union's survival!'

She looked at him with hostility in her eyes and declared, 'No.'

He was standing up, angrily glaring at the view screen now, 'And how long do you think Earth will last without the protection of the Galactic Union?'

'You fool! It's the Galactic Union that's trying to destroy us! Look around you! And my decision is hardly voluntary. Don't you understand, *I was included in the activation of the Terran psychic network.* I can no more turn my back on Earth now than I can stop breathing.'

He stopped and then said, 'I'm coming over to your ship.'

'Why?'

'This is something we need to discuss in person.'

'For all the good it will do you. Your presence on this ship will not change the situation, Dom.'

'I need to talk to you in person.'

'I see no reason for you to come over.'

Dom looked thoughtfully at the elf collapsed at her feet, 'Your elvish friend will die soon if you do not help him. Do you know how to do that?'

Laura didn't even bother to tell him that Zokar was not really her friend, just a temporary ally: it was too complicated to explain. She looked down at Zokar, his face as pale now as his hair and admitted, 'No.'

'Then I will be there in a few minutes. Keep him in stasis until I arrive or you will lose him.'

She nodded, exhausted herself. She concentrated on holding the stasis effect around Zokar.

# CHAPTER TWENTY-FOUR

Dom arrived in the shuttle and moved through the still forms around him, meeting his sister's eyes with his black ones. He knelt next to Zokar and held his hand over the wound in Zokar's side. Laura watched as the wound healed up and stared as Dom gathered light? Energy? All around her tall dark-haired brother, light gathered and was sucked into Zokar's body. Dom nodded to her and she released the stasis and Zokar stirred.

'Let's get him to the medical bay,' Dom suggested and picked up the heavy elf like he was a child. He headed over to the lift and entered it, Laura trailing behind. Her instincts were screaming at her to go back to the unconscious Trudi, but instincts were also telling her that Trudi would be much better off, if Dom did not know who she was.

'How are you doing all this?' Laura wondered, as Zokar blinked sleepily up at Dom but then passed out.

'Matter-energy conversion, gravitic manipulation, all things you would have been thoroughly trained in, had you been raised by your real family,' Dom said.

The lift was moving for several seconds too long, but Laura didn't notice, until too late, when the doors opened into the shuttle bay, and Dom reached out to her and squeezed a tranquillising gas bubble right under her nose. Laura slumped, and he held her with one arm and Zokar with the other, holding the guards in stasis around them as he carted his heavy load back onto the shuttle.

Once space-borne again, he signalled the Reingold bridge. The view screen came up, with the furious face of Elesk glaring at him, 'Return our commander immediately, and the Empress's daughter,' she scowled.

'No. What are you going to do, fire on me? I have your commander and the Empress's daughter on board this shuttle.'

Elesk swore in old Elvish.

Dom returned to his ship and kept Laura and Zokar sedated as he led his flotilla of five ships away towards the Galactic Core. He wasn't taking any chances, after all he had his sister on board, *now*.

He knew that if and when he returned that the Terran uprising would have been quelled and the planet Earth destroyed. Nobody defied the Union as the Terrans had done and got away with it.

# CHAPTER TWENTY-FIVE

Trudi regained consciousness and then wished she hadn't. Her head was throbbing painfully, 'Laura?'

'She is gone,' a quiet voice said beside her. Trudi looked in horror at Elesk's cool silver face.

'Gone?' Trudi whispered and felt something awaken within her. Was it anger?

'Taken by her brother, into the Core,' Elesk answered.

'What brother?' Trudi asked, confused.

'Domhan Keallach, her twin brother, from the Galactic Union,' Elesk explained.

'Damn,' Trudi said, 'What are we doing?'

'Damage control. We are in fact, low on power, without full navigational capability, waiting to be blown up, I would say,' Elesk sighed.

'Do we have viewers?' Trudi asked.

'Yes,' Elesk waved an arm at the neat line of Galactic Union battle cruisers before the two remaining battle cruisers that McCosker had commandeered. McCosker's ships were pitted and burnt, floating between the Union ships and the delicate circle of blue that was Earth.

Trudi struggled to her feet, and asked, 'What are they doing?'

'They are conferring with their prisoners.'

'Why are they lined up like that?' Trudi asked.

Elesk shrugged and Trudi realised that the elven woman was injured herself, and not quite with it.

Elesk said, 'They are probably lining up in preparation for the planet sterilization procedure.'

The two women met each other's eyes, Elesk's dull and sad, Trudi's horrified.

An idea was forming in Trudi's head and she whispered a word which Elesk did not understand, then asked, 'How much power do we have left in this old rig?'

'Enough to go into low hyperdrive, just. Not enough to get us out of the Solar system. Why?'

'Enough to cloak us?' Trudi asked.

'Only for a few minutes,' Elesk replied, growing more curious and alert, 'But there is no point in running, we would not get very far.'

'I wasn't thinking of running. Can you drive the Reingold, Elesk?'

Elesk raised her eyebrows, 'Yes. What exactly do you have in mind?'

'There's an old Earth game...' Trudi began to explain.

Several minutes later, over on the Earth-controlled ships, McCosker was snarling at the Union Admiral on his view screen, 'So what now, you blow us up, then go for the planet?'

'Precisely.'

'You arseholes,' McCosker said, then glanced to the left of his view screen and went quiet.

The General's eyes naturally followed McCosker's, just in time to glimpse the Reingold, coming out of silent running, only a few metres from his ship.

'Take that, you Union bastards!' Trudi screamed, as the massive Reingold rammed into the first of the neatly lined up Galactic Union battle cruisers before McCosker.

Explosions flowered from the Reingold and the first battle cruiser, which was impaled on the nose of the Reingold. Then the Reingold re-entered hyperdrive and the rest of the twelve battle cruisers exploded one by one, the Reingold and its newly acquired hood ornament taking them down in rapid succession.

McCosker cheered wildly. Then they all stared transfixed, because the Reingold, protected by the first battle cruiser jammed onto its hull at the nose, emerged largely unscathed after ramming the battle cruisers. It turned back to drift into orbit around Earth. On the Reingold, internal bulkheads slammed down against the loss of air from the damage at its front end, protecting the big ship's atmosphere supply.

McCosker's view screen changed to show the stunned face of Trudi St James, who said to the terrified Elesk beside her, 'Hey, look at that, we're still alive!' She burst out laughing.

McCosker, Nick, Ryan and Karl stood in awestruck silence and looked at the laughing dark-haired girl on their screen.

'You guys are on our side, right?' Trudi asked.

McCosker and his team nodded vigorously, and McCosker said, 'Hell, yeah. Who in the name of creation are you, girl?'

'Trudi,' she grinned, 'Trudi St James, of Earth.'

'This 'dominoes', it is an interesting game,' Elesk smiled, before fainting at Trudi's feet.

# CHAPTER TWENTY-SIX

Laura stared at the huge brown eyes before her. She could not fathom that this dark-haired woman could be their mother. Yet there was something in the perfect shape of her face, the rounded almond shape of those eyes, something about the feel of the woman.

A mind that looked into her very soul, a quiet voice that started to steal her heart before she had said more than a few words, a gentleness that warmed Laura with each word that was spoken.

But she listened to the measured words of her mother and began to wonder.

'The people of Terra are a violent and dangerous breed, my child. You have grown up with them so you do not see this, but it is clear to us what a threat they are to the civilised Galaxies.'

'My lady,' Laura said, following Dom's lead in addressing this strange, warm yet distant figure, 'I can no more betray my people than Dom can. How are we to resolve this?'

'You both want peace, then declare peace.'

'It will never stick. My people are not puppets. Even if I were to take every one of their minds and control them individually, I do need to sleep. And when I sleep, they will go out and fight.'

'She is correct, my lady,' Dom agreed, 'The Terrans are deadly and they do not trust easily. Our first act in their eyes, was to threaten to destroy them. Any pleas for peace on my part, or even Laura's part, will simply be seen as subterfuge. Not even Laura can get them to trust us now.'

'I can lead them, but I cannot control them, my lady.'

Arlene looked at them both, feeling an odd warmth in her soul. These twins were the best of her children. She was amazed that Dom had found his sister alive and well, and delighted that his first act was to bring her back to see her mother.

'You are both good children. Work this out. Your goals are the same and it is merely a matter of applying logic to the situation to deduce the best method for achieving the outcome of peace that you both aspire to. Am I correct?'

They both looked at her helplessly. She continued, 'Dom.... Laura, do not let this galaxy be torn apart by this. Do not let our home become a playground for the dogs of war. I have worked too long and too hard to see everything we have all worked for, come to nothing. We have had no Ruling Pair for too long, and our people are tired and frightened. There are new threats to this galaxy that even you two are not aware of. *We need to be united.*'

Dom stepped forward instinctively, and knelt at his mother's feet. She put a fond hand upon his head and looked at Laura. Laura shook her head, 'I'm sorry, my lady, I don't even know you,'

'Look inside yourself and you will find that you do,' Arlene advised gently.

Laura shook her head, and Arlene was shocked at the wariness in her, 'You are like a deer in the forest, my child, you watch every place at once, and trust no-one.'

'She was raised on Earth, mother,' Dom said, 'She has grown up like a wild animal.'

'And yet, such power lies within your heart, my daughter. What will you do with it?' Arlene asked.

'Survive,' Laura whispered and turned to walk away.

'You must do more than that. You must lead your people now. All of them. It is your birth right, true, but it is also your responsibility. You cannot accept the privileges of your royal birth, without accepting the responsibilities that go hand in hand with those privileges.'

'Privileges?' Laura rounded on them, 'Privileges? You call it a privilege to be so ill-cared for that I was kidnapped, and then left for dead for twenty two years on a prison planet? You call it a privilege to be drugged, kidnapped again, shot at, and then told I must 'serve my people' even if that is to the detriment and possible destruction of those innocent savages who raised me? You must have a very different view of privilege from mine. I am returning to my home.'

'Very well, we will not try to stop you. But remember, daughter, that all the resources of this Union are at your disposal, should you ever need them.'

'Pah!' Laura exclaimed as she strode towards the door.

Dom looked conflicted, but his mother pushed him away with a gentle hand. 'You go keep an eye on her. Don't lose her again!'

Dom planted a hasty kiss on his mother's forehead and ran after Laura. He caught up with her a few turns down the corridor.

'Laura, wait!'

She strode along, 'So what is she, high-elvish? That would explain the complete indifference,'

'My God, you're cold. That's your mother! Twenty-two years and you can't spare a hug?' He grabbed her arm and spun her angrily around, then stopped and saw the tears flooding the normally impassive grey eyes. Dom gathered her in his arms, 'Oh, hey,'

She sobbed into her brother's arms and said, 'Dom, she's a stranger. I don't even know her. I would have passed her in the street and not known her. I had thought she would be like me, look more like me,'

'If you're talking about physical appearance, you take after our father.'

She straightened up, 'But you see, Dom, I've always been the silver-haired one, it's what made me different from the rest of the humans on Earth, and I guess I imagined, when I found out I was an alien, that my parents would both look more, I don't know, alien. I didn't think my mother would look so human. It's weird, but over the last few weeks I've built up a picture in my mind, of what she would look like. She looks so different from what I expected.'

'You didn't know me, either,' he suggested softly.

'Yeah, but the first thing you did was save my ass. And that's different. Everyone knows there's a twin thingy.'

'A thingy?' Dom was amused, but then serious again, 'But what about the mother-daughter thingy?'

'All she cares about is what I can do for her goddamned Union, Dom. She doesn't care about me and when it gets right down to brass knuckles she doesn't care about Earth, either.'

'That's not true.'

'She didn't even ask how I was. Didn't even ask, if my planet was still in one piece, my people okay!'

Dom stared at her and started to laugh softly, rocking her in his arms.

'What?' she demanded, 'What is so damned funny?'

'You say all she cares for is her goddamned Union and then in the next breath, you are expressing your main concern, your planet and your people.'

'So?'

'Isn't it just the same thing? It may be on a different scale, but aren't you exactly like her?'

'That's ridiculous!' She pulled out of his embrace and strode towards the lift that would take them up and out of the secure compound.

'How?' he demanded, jogging to keep up with her.

'It just is.'

'That's not even an attempt at reason!'

'I don't care. I'm going home.'

'Okay, but I'm coming with you.'

She stopped dead, and he collided with her, swearing.

'What?' she asked, incredulous.

'Our mother told me to look after you.'

'You have got to be kidding. How the hell do you think the people of Earth are going to react to me when I turn up with a Union Admiral in tow?'

'Not my problem.'

'Thanks a lot. Dom, go back to your mother. You can't help me protect Earth. You would be fighting your own people. Could you honestly aim your turrets at a Union ship?'

Dom stared at her, then hung his head, 'But I promised her I would look after you.'

'And I'm telling you, you're barking up the wrong tree. I don't need looking after. And unless you're willing to gun down your own people in defence of my planet, I can't have you at my side. You would be a distraction and I would worry that you would stop me from doing what is necessary to protect Earth.' She sighed, 'Dom, I will go to Earth and set up their defences. Once I am sure that Earth has a safe perimeter set up, I promise, I will return and try to help you establish peace here at the Core. In the meantime, the best thing you can do is remain here and start working on that peace.'

Back in her chambers, Arlene waited. Eventually, in the silence, a gleam of silver eyes appeared, and a tall, silver-haired creature appeared. He was taller than even Zokar Rizian, but had the same colouring, and the pointed ears and six fingers of the old-elvish. He stepped quietly over to Arlene and said quietly, in a deep voice,

'She is so like you, my love.'

'You think? She seemed…. aloof, distant,' Arlene replied sadly.

Ataar Rizian put his arms around his wife and said, 'She will come around. No-one could resist you.'

'But Ataar, the Union needs her and it needs Dom. Now they are both on their way back to Earth, and we have no-one to unite the warring factions within the Union.'

'We have them.'

'You know they need to be here at the Core, both of them.'

Ataar Rizian looked thoughtful and pondered, 'Do they?'

'How are they going to rule the Galactic Union from Earth? The Terrans already hate us, anyway. With good reason, I might add.'

'I don't know. Perhaps if they start at the Rim?'

'What and build the Union from there?' She looked pensive, then shook her head, 'There's still the matter of the Admirals threatening to destroy Earth. Those Terrans have no reason to trust anything about the Union. We set Earth up as a prison planet and threatened to kill them all.'

'Mmmmm, not our finest hour,' Ataar smiled, stroking her hair.

'You're unbelievable.'

'Hmmm. It is a complex problem in logic. Forgive me, I sometimes expect too much of you,'

She looked indignant and said, 'And what is that supposed to mean?'

'It means, that it may take a few days' thought, to figure out a solution. But, my dear wife, I am sure a solution will present itself.'

'I hope so. I hope so, Ataar.' She looked out the door that Laura had exited minutes before.

He leaned over and kissed her gently, then said, 'Don't worry, Dom will look after her.'

Just then, Dom walked back in the door.

'Ataar!'

'Dom. I thought you were going with your sister?'

'She has promised to set up Earth's defences, then to return and join us.'

Arlene sighed, 'It is as much as we can hope for.'

'You brought a prisoner back with you,' Ataar Rizian said.

'What do you want me to do with him?' Dom's question was directed at Arlene.

'Release him to the custody of his father,' Arlene said, glancing quietly at Ataar Rizian, who nodded gravely in gratitude.

'I don't think he will stay. Laura told me that he has a ship back near Earth, and a captain that is lost on Earth, whom he wishes to rescue,' Dom said.

Ataar stared at Dom, 'Zokar is loyal to this captain?'

Dom looked at the floor and nodded.

'He will not be of any help to us, then,' Ataar sighed.

'I'm not so sure, Ataar,' Dom said, 'The captain is a merchant with the Galactic Trade Alliance. They were searching for Laura when they went to Earth. He is human, but not Terran. He has also been stranded there these last few weeks, he is probably terrified of Earth by now.'

'We can only hope,' Ataar sighed.

# CHAPTER TWENTY-SEVEN

The triumph after the Reingold rammed the twelve Union ships was short lived, for the Galactic Union seemed to have an endless supply of battle cruisers. The incoming Union ships had apparently woken up to the dangers of the Terran group mind, and were using guerrilla tactics, regrouping together at a distance, then spreading out and attacking simultaneously from several points at once, darting in and firing and darting out, always staying just out of range of the group-mind's reach. With ten more ships circling them like darting vultures, the three ships occupied by the Terran humans were virtually immobilised, and try as they might they could not get far enough away from Earth for the general's comfort.

McCosker was staring out past the three newly scanned Union ships that had their guns aimed directly at the battle-ravaged battle cruiser which he was trying to pilot. The helm was sluggish and the ship floated in space like a drunken sailor.

He could see something behind the other vessels, and it was puzzling him. It looked like a cloud of grey mist, but you don't get mist in space.

Then the grey mist clarified itself into a huge group of grey dots. The Union ships spun away from McCosker's vessel and fled as the grey dots enlarged into a flotilla of small, rounded ships....

'What the hell?' he wondered.

Then Nick said quietly into the silence around them.... 'Sir, look!' as the face of one of the Grey aliens appeared on their screen.

'General McCoskerrr,' said the tallest of a group of greys in a strange, stretched out accent, 'We have been monitorweeng your transmissions. We come to assist you.'

McCosker felt the air escape from his lungs and realised that he had been holding his breath since the Union ships had trained their guns on his vessel.

'Man, are we glad to see you guys?' he smiled.

'What are they?' Nick asked in alarm, seeing about fifty white dots appear behind the grey ships.

'It iis, the Fey,' the grey alien advised.

'Wow,' McCosker said, 'The cavalry!'

Nick sighed in relief. The battle hadn't been going well for the Earth forces. Even with their new-found psychic unity, the Terran humans had been fighting a desperate battle which they had all felt was a losing one.

# CHAPTER TWENTY-EIGHT

Zokar's head was pounding, and that was what woke him up. He stirred, but stilled warily and felt something hard under him, a bench? He felt around, barely moving his fingers to explore the surface beneath him and confirmed his suspicions. He opened his eyes, then sighed and sat up as he saw the vertical lines of light which indicated that he was in a prison cell. He inspected his surroundings. He was still in the clothes that he had been wearing when he lost consciousness on the bridge of the Reingold. He wondered how long ago that had been, hours, or days?

He was relieved to be alone as he did not feel like coping with a cell mate. He sat still for a moment, and then felt a strange sensation in his feet. They were tingling beneath him, as though the nerves were reacting to something. He placed his hand flat upon the surface of the bench and realised with shock what was making his feet feel odd; there was no vibration in the floor.

Zokar had spent all of his adult life on board star ships of one description or another, and he was used to the familiar hum and vibration of a ship's motors beneath his feet. Instead there was gravity and he took a moment to assess its nature. Gravity could have many feels; rotary artificial, the more expensive quantum generated artificial, lunar and the solid, unvarying pull that is planetary gravity. This was unmistakably planetary gravity.

So, he was on a planet somewhere, not Earth, because Earth did not have the technology for force field bars as he had seen here. Of course, it was possible that this was a clandestine base on Earth, but no, he realised, the gravity was too heavy.

A door opened and he realised with a thump of his heart where he was, for beyond the door there was a window, and beyond that was the night sky, from which flooded a wash of starlight so intense, so bright, that it could only mean one thing. He was near the Galactic Core.

Zokar groaned. He was in a Union prison.

'Stand back,' the guard ordered and Zokar did so, but realising that the man was armed, alone and not very wary, Zokar waited until the guard bent down to place his food on the small round table near his sleeping bench, then gave the guard a sudden knockout blow to the back of his neck with both hands. He divested the man of his uniform and donned it himself, including the laser disruptor and headed out of the cell, checking for guards as he went.

It struck him as ironic, that a week ago, his actions tonight would have earned him banishment to the very planet that he desperately wanted to get back to. But now, there was a battle line between him and Earth. A battle line which he had to cross.

He knocked out three more guards and managed to steal an air bike, in which someone had left their card. The bike's custodian raced out when he heard it power up, but as the giant beefy man came up to the vehicle, Zokar kicked it down and up into gear, then gunned it. He had seen the lights of a small village about twenty kilometres from the place where he had been held and he knew he would be able to get food there. The only trouble was that in some areas of the Galactic Core they did not use money. A small rabbit-like animal crossed the highway before him and he considered briefly the idea of hunting for his food, but it was too time-consuming.

Zokar ditched the bike in a dam about two kilometres out of the village and walked in through the cultivated paddocks. No savage animals came to attack him, and no snakes or other poisonous creatures were to be seen. There are some things to be said for the Core, he thought. Zokar heaved a sigh of relief when he saw the marketplace, it was possible that a culture this close to the Core might have been credit or savings card only. He would however, still have to steal the money or steal the food.

In the end, it came down to luck. As Zokar walked past a stall selling nuts and dried meats, the small child belonging to the owner fell and skinned her knee, and in the fuss Zokar managed to slip a plentiful supply of food under his uniform without being noticed.

He headed for a quiet spot and ate, because he had been very hungry when the guard back at the prison had brought him his meal. Eventually with a full stomach and a decent supply of dried food in his pockets, he headed out to find a spaceport.

He followed the heavier traffic and came to a thriving port. At one point he had managed to swing on the back of an air-truck when it stopped for traffic and caught a lift undetected.

Strangely enough, he found it fairly easy to steal a ship, most civilians did not have the expertise to fly a ship, let alone control and navigate it safely into and out of hyperdrive. The ships stood out in the open and the guards were neglectful because crime at the Galactic Core was almost non-existent due to harsh penalties.

Zokar began to breathe again as the ship soared out from the small planet's atmosphere. He felt the oppressive pull of planetary gravity release his frame, and get replaced by the more variable gentle tug of artificial gravity. The breezy echoes of planetary distances faded and were replaced by the familiar thrum of engines. Zokar had grown up on star ships, and although there were some aspects of being outdoors and planet side that he loved, he never quite got over the feeling of being most at home on board a ship.

He took his bearings from the local constellations and sighed. It was a long way back out to the Perseus Arm, then to the Rim.

He throttled the ship up to maximum hyperdrive, at a speed which would overtax the engines if he kept it up for too long, but Zokar did not care. The ship could burn out for all he cared: so long as it got him back to Earth before it did.

The ship was fully fuelled but did not have a cloaking system. Zokar resigned himself to many sleepless hours of travel before him, because he would have to watch for other ships. He tightened his lips and thought of Shiva, lost and in danger on Earth and his resolve firmed. He started planning his trip to take him around the back routes of the Union and back to the buffer zone and Earth.

# CHAPTER TWENTY-NINE

It was two days later that the news arrived at the Core that the Greys from Andromeda had turned out in force to protect Earth and that the Fey had switched their allegiance to the Terrans. The Union now faced a real threat from the Outer Rim.

Arlene gave the order to start mustering the fleet.

Dom stormed into her chambers, 'I just heard. You can't be serious.'

'The Greys of Andromeda are not part of the Union, Domhan. The Fey have defected. The Terrans are now a real threat to Galactic peace.'

'What because their friends saved them from us? Are you mad? We attacked Earth!'

'Earth is part of our jurisdiction. They have rebelled, gathered allies and now must be put down,' Arlene said, looking irritated.

'Mother, it's not fair!'

'I will act as I must to preserve the peace,' she told him angrily.

'You could try talking to them! I don't suppose it has occurred to you to send a diplomatic delegation?' he asked, pacing up and down as he spoke.

'To those savages?'

'How can you be so bigoted?' he demanded, pausing in his pacing to stare at her.

'You are not being objective. Your sister is involved and you have lost perspective.'

'I'm going to see my sister, see if I can sort this out,' Dom said, his voice decisive now.

'What makes you think you will succeed where you failed before?' Arlene asked.

'I have to try. Where's the fleet?'

'Deployed. They will be twenty light years out by now.'

'Shit,' he exclaimed and stalked out, heading for his ship. If he was going to get to Laura before the fleet, he would have to hurry.

# CHAPTER THIRTY

The third battle cruiser that had originally arrived at Earth had indeed shot halfway to the next star system, Alpha Centauri, due to its current occupants' indifferent knowledge of hyperdrive navigation. The three university students floated in the air above the near-mesmerised bridge crew.

'Mikey, what's this?' Kim said.

'What's what, Kim?' Mikey said, drifting across to her to look down with her at the readout she was surveying.

'Well, this news feed, it's about that guy that saved Earth, I think. Zokar Rizian? That's him, right?' Kim asked.

'Yeah, that's right. What's happened?' Mikey said.

'Well, I've figured out the translator and it looks like he's been arrested,' she said.

'Arrested? For what?' Mikey asked.

'Um taking two people to the Galactic Core that he wasn't supposed to, and protecting felons. Hang on, that's Earth!'

'What?' Joe asked drifting over to join them. All three hovered over the readout.

'It, I'm not sure if I'm reading this right, but it looks like Earth people are considered felons,' Kim said.

'Yeah, you're reading it right,' Mikey replied.

They looked at each other, then Joe turned to Mikey, 'You know, that isn't right. They shouldn't be arresting this guy. He saved our planet, for Christ's sake!'

'Well, what can we do about it?' Mikey asked.

Joe thought about it for a moment, then suggested, 'Maybe we could try to rescue him?'

'How? We'd be stopped as soon as we got into their territory,' Mikey said.

'Would we? We are in one of their ships,' Joe said.

Kim looked thoughtful, then smiled, 'We might just get away with it.'

'Come on, let's figure out how to cloak this thing,' Mikey

grinned.

'Are you sure we should be doing this?' Kim asked. She looked around the big bridge, wondering about the safety of the crew.

'Well, who else is going to do it? We're the guys for the job, Kim.'

'I guess so. Wait, they don't have the death penalty or anything, do they?' She looked into the view screen again. 'You know, it says that transportation to Earth has been temporarily suspended and prisoners are being taken to this little planet near the middle of the Galaxy. But, the way they're talking about Earth, it sounds like it's a prison colony. Like Australia was.'

Joe peered at the new schematic that she had brought up, 'That can't be right. You must be reading it wrong, Kim. Anyway, it doesn't mention a death penalty, only mind filtering? What the hell is that?'

'It doesn't sound good, does it?' Mikey said, 'Come on, let's go get this Zokar guy. Our planet owes him one.'

# CHAPTER THIRTY-ONE

Zokar had not slept for three days and he was getting antsy.

A merchant ship contacted him and he presented himself as a tourist.

The captain of the merchant ship, a rangy middle-aged woman with suspicious eyes, commented, 'You are far from the usual tourist destinations, stranger.'

'What's the point of having my own ship if I don't use it to go off the beaten track?' Zokar demanded.

'You do not seem very relaxed for someone who is holidaying.'

'Relaxed? Of course I'm not relaxed! Tell your gunner to unlock his weapons systems from my ship. Then I will relax,' Zokar snapped. He realised that he was doing a bad job of acting like a tourist, but he was tired and hungry. The ship had been well fuelled, but low on food. The prospect of one more bowl of rice did not improve his mood.

She stared at him, 'How do you know our weapons are locked on to your ship? Do you have battle grade scanning systems?'

Of course I do, surely you don't think I would venture this far out into space without defences?' Zokar asked, forcing himself to lean back in his chair and look relaxed.

'Oh? Are you carrying valuables?'

Zokar was getting an insight into how other ships felt when they came in contact with him and Shiva on the Reingold. He stared into the avaricious eyes of the captain, and shook his head, 'Only my precious hide.'

They left him alone, no doubt after scanning his ship for the hoped-for valuables, which were non-existent. Zokar breathed a sigh of relief and powered on past them, setting the ship's course for the Perseus arm. It was further than he thought.

It was not until he had dodged pirates, stayed awake for a further three nights to navigate a huge asteroid belt that was not on his star maps and travelled for another four nights, that he came to an awful and embarrassing realisation. He was used to the

Reingold's massive fuel reserves, which allowed plenty of leeway for such delays. This small ship with its tiny fuel reserve had no such luxury, and he had run out of fuel. He had enough to keep life support and deflectors on for a week, but not enough to make another hyperdrive jump. Zokar put his head in his hands and considered the least embarrassing way to call for help, which was now his only option. The trouble was, calling for help out here would probably result in him contacting the last people he wanted to know where he was; the Galactic Union. He sighed and set the distress beacon anyway.

It was two days later when Zokar's worst fears were realised, a Union Battle Cruiser came out of hyperdrive a few hundred metres in front of him and a voice said, 'Zokar Rizian?'

Zokar sighed at the behemoth, which dwarfed his little vessel. They would be scanning him and no doubt knew who he was, there was no point denying his identity. He closed his eyes and waited for the blast which would obliterate him. The Union soldiers had no reason to spare his life.

At least death will come quickly, Zokar thought and an odd calm came over him. He supposed his life should be flashing before his eyes, but it did not. The only thought that came to his mind, was regret that Shiva would not know that Zokar had tried to save him. I'm sorry, Shiva, he thought. 'Goodbye, my old friend,' he whispered, then hit the communications button, 'Yes, it is Zokar Rizian here.'

A ridiculously young face with a shock of bright orange hair popped onto his screen and grinned at him, 'Zokar Rizian, we're from Earth and we've come to rescue you.'

Zokar stared at the face before him, taking in the lack of uniform, the cheerful grin, and his mind took a few seconds to absorb the information. Then he found himself smiling for the first time in a long while. Dammit, he was really getting to like these Terrans.

Being an elf, he suppressed his smile quickly and nodded 'Well, thank you.'

When his ship had docked and he had found his way onto the bridge, Mikey, Kim and Joe greeted him with curious eyes.

Zokar said gravely, 'I am indebted to you for your assistance.'

Mikey asked, 'How did you get all the way out here? We were heading to the Core to get you out.'

Zokar stared at him, 'Why would you do that?'

'Because you saved Earth and they stuck you in jail for it. That's not fair,' Mikey said.

Zokar wondered about the Terran sense of right and wrong. The more he had to do with Terrans, the more he liked them.

Mikey, Kim and Joe asked Zokar many questions on the way back. None of them, Zokar realised, would ever have met an alien, so he answered their questions patiently as they turned the battle cruiser and headed at full speed back to Earth. He could still hardly wrap his mind around his good fortune.

Zokar was happy to see the intact Reingold in orbit around Earth. Then he leaned forward in his chair and looked more closely at the nose of his ship and his head tilted in puzzlement.

When he contacted the Reingold, he was surprised to see the pale but determined face of Trudi St James appear on his view screen.

'Trudi? What are you doing?'

'Oh nothing, just trying to protect Earth while you lot blow each other to bits out here. Where have you been, Zokar? Laura came back a few days ago and she's hardly talking to anyone.'

'I will shuttle over. Is, is that a *battle cruiser*, on the nose of my ship?'

'Oh yeah. Sorry about that,' she said, 'We had a bit of an incident.'

He stared at her, his mouth open.

# CHAPTER THIRTY-TWO

Shiva was hunting, using his handmade spear. He had fashioned himself a rough shield out of a piece of corrugated tin he had found. He stepped quietly along the sandy path, puzzled. He could smell iron. He cleared a corner of the trail and came face to face with the silent snarl of a big cat standing over a fresh deer kill. Shiva did not know what sort of animal the big cat was, only that she had large teeth and bad intentions, and stood almost up to his shoulder. She launched herself at him and he crouched on one knee and thrust his shield and spear upwards, bracing the butt of the spear on the ground at his side. There were several horrible feline shrieks as the savage cat convulsed impaled on the spear and clawed at face of his shield. The cat stilled and he pushed the feline's body to the side and stood up.

He had been lucky to escape being a side dish for the deer. He stepped forward, wiping spatters of blood from his face and automatically spitting in case some had got into his mouth. To his surprise when he spat, a similar sound came back out of the bramble bushes beside the dead deer.

Shiva crouched and lowered his shield, but then two silky kittens came tumbling out of the bushes, play-fighting with each other. One was black with chocolate brown eyes. The other had the golden colouring of its dam, but none of the donut-shaped markings or stripes that the mother had. It was a dark gold all over, but had strange deep blue eyes, possibly due to the same colour dilution gene which had removed the markings from its coat. Shiva stared at the cubs and realised that they must be very young, because they rolled against his feet, stood up and gazed at him curiously. Older cubs would have reacted with fear and suspicion and been aware of their dead mother. These two were too young to know fear.

He reached down and rubbed gently around the black cub's pointed ears, and it purred and rubbed up against his ankles. The golden cub, sensing that it was missing out, tried to climb Shiva's leg. The big warlord laughed as its claws became entangled in the laces on his leather boots. He gently extricated it and picked it up, then scooped up its littermate and placed them near the kill. They alternated between savaging the kill and each other, eating and purring around him as he sliced clean meat out of the fresh kill. He slung the meat over his shoulder to make his way back to his camp.

The camp was only a mile or so away, but he had not expected the little black cub to follow him home. The golden cub trotted along behind, occasionally meowing a protest at the heat and the long journey. When they reached the camp, Shiva poured them some water. They gulped the water then promptly fell asleep in the warm grass in front of his shelter.

Hours later when Shiva settled in his shelter for the evening he found himself being used as a security blanket and hot-water bottle for the two newly orphaned creatures. They tucked themselves in under his armpits and purred him out of his sleep, succeeding a few times.

Shiva was not the type to adopt pets, but the two little cubs gave him no choice. He was their surrogate mother, because he had killed their real mother. Perhaps it was that sense of guilt that stopped him from simply dispatching them and eating them. Perhaps it was simply because he didn't mind the purring, the warmth and the feel of another creature beside him in this frightening place. And perhaps he thought of their mother and realised that two such large predators in his corner might just give him the edge he needed to survive on this savage planet.

Over the next few weeks the little cubs grew rapidly, and he let them eat with him whenever he hunted. Sometimes they would sleep while he went out, but more and more often, they would trot beside him, the black silky one first, watching Shiva and the trail ahead, the golden cub trailing behind, trotting and looking around more. He gave them names for their colours, Gan for the black one and Ghrian for the golden one, whose coat gleamed like Earth's golden sun.

One morning, Shiva was surprised to find a small pile of beheaded rabbits littering the grass in front of the shelter when he woke up. The golden cub was still sleeping and the black cub was sitting outside, licking his paws and looking smug. Shiva approached carefully, not sure what sort of reception he would get if he approached Gan's kill. To his surprise, Gan picked up the largest rabbit's body and dumped it at his feet when he exited the shelter.

He rubbed the half-grown cat's ears admiringly and said, 'You are earning your keep already, my little friend.' Gan settled down on his side and batted at Shiva's hands with sheathed claws, purring up a storm, as though he understood what Shiva had said to him.

Ghrian, the golden cub, was given the same generous treatment by his littermate when he emerged sleepily from the shelter. He lay down and tore at the raw meat of his rabbit gift, then purred loudly for a while and fell back to sleep.

Shiva, relieved of the duty of hunting for breakfast, fried up strips of rabbit meat and made himself some black coffee, a luxury which he had found in a deserted farm shed a few days earlier. It was a relaxing morning and as he lay back against his now-regular pillow, Gan's purring stomach, and gazed up at the blue sky, he started to understand why the Earth creatures loved their planet with such a passion.

He had wondered why the Terrans tolerated the sharp teeth and demanding appetites of the cats and dogs they took into their homes and he could not understand how the humans could sleep at night with dangerous animals roaming freely about their homes, but now he was starting to understand. If they grew up with you, if they trusted you from an early age, these fierce creatures became your most valuable allies, protectors of your home, loyal as only predators could be. Shiva thought of Zokar and realised that his relationship with the elf had been similar to his relationship with these two creatures. Zokar had been an apex predator, too, in his own right, but once they had learned to trust each other Zokar had become the most valuable ally that Shiva had ever had.

Shiva sighed and rubbed Gan's ears. He still missed the elf and wondered where he was and if he was still alive.

Gan's purring was growing louder and louder and Shiva realised that the big cub was growling, not purring. Shiva heard a strange noise from over the ridge near his cave, and put a restraining hand on the scruff of Gan's neck. He snuck over towards the ridge and peered over it.

To his surprise, a group of Grey aliens and humans were gathered about the clearing below them. Shiva shrank back into the bushes behind the ridge, pulling Gan with him. He nearly jumped out his skin when he felt something cold and wet against his ankle, but realised it was Ghrian, who had woken up and come to join them. Ghrian sensed their furtiveness and crouched low, peering out of the bushes with Shiva and Gan.

A Grey alien walked away from the group in their general direction. It was an unprepossessing creature, about a metre tall, dark grey, completely hairless, with a large oval shaped head and enormous dark eyes. It was a harmless enough looking creature, with no claws or talons to speak of and no great strength or fighting ability. Why then, did all humans react with such terror to its presence? It stared in their direction for a minute and Shiva felt an undefined terror, a vague sense of danger, of being stalked and hunted, which crawled into the back of his mind. The big cats were strangely silent beside him.

A shuttle hummed over the horizon and distracted the Grey, which went back to the group. The shuttle landed in the clearing and the Greys seemed to herd the humans with them aboard the shuttle, like cattle. Shiva was puzzled and even though he had been going to call out to the Greys and ask for help, something about the whole situation stopped him cold.

The vehicle rose up into the treetops with a rush of displaced air and turned and floated away. Shiva watched it until it was out of sight, a tiny white dot in the blue sky, then sat down and wondered about his own strange reaction to such a harmless species of alien.

'I'm an idiot,' he told the cats, but he knew that he could no more have called out to the Greys for help than he could have cut his own throat.

He noticed however, that Gan and Ghrian both had silent snarls on their faces as they watched the sky where the shuttle had disappeared. After that both cats gave the area where the Greys had gathered a wide berth and stayed closer to Shiva.

# CHAPTER THIRTY-THREE

'What are they scanning for?' Laura asked, pausing in her slow pacing of the Reingold's bridge to look at the three technicians lined up beside Elesk at her scanning board.

'Some of our people are still lost on the planet below,' Zokar replied grimly.

'Why can't you find them?' Laura asked.

'The crew that remain down there are pure bred humans. They are indistinguishable from the other seven billion purebred humans on your planet,' sighed Zokar.

'Including your friend Shiva?'

'The captain, yes,' he said stiffly.

She looked thoughtful for a while then said, 'Zokar, when I was on the Fey ship they were scanning their own power levels to make sure they would make it up to orbit. They scanned me. There was a power fluctuation around me when we started moving away from the suppression generator. Is it possible that all Terran humans would have that, now that the generator's gone?'

Zokar stared at Laura for a long second, then clapped her on the back, nearly knocking her off her feet, 'And our people would not!'

He turned to Elesk who had already recalibrated her scanners with the new information. Zokar said, 'I just hope you're not the only one, Laura.'

Trudi asked, 'But I don't understand. How are you going to find Shiva if he gives no power reading?'

Laura said, 'He'll have a life form reading, Tru. Anyone with just a life form reading couldn't be Terran, so that leaves the lost crew members.'

'Detection by a process of elimination,' Zokar smiled, his fingers flying over the board in front of him.

'If you're so clever, why didn't you think of that?' Trudi asked Zokar.

'Shut up and stand still,' Zokar growled at Trudi.

'I beg your pardon?' Trudi said incredulously.

Laura put a gentle hand on her arm and said, 'You're a Terran human. He's using you as a reference point.'

'Oh,' Trudi said.

'Got it! She has it!' Zokar exclaimed, then leaned over Elesk's shoulder to the main scanning board and started working, his hands moving so fast Trudi could hardly see them. The life form readings were tiny red dots and now little blue circles appeared around most of them.

'There! There, and there!' Elesk pointed out three red dots without blue circles.

Zokar's elvish eyes scanned and memorised the map.

Trudi leaned forward to look at the scanner and asked him, 'How will you know which one is Shiva?'

But when she and the others turned around, Zokar was gone. Laura ran after him.

# CHAPTER THIRTY-FOUR

Zokar landed with a thump. He folded up his antigravity net.

He scrambled in along the tunnel on his belly. Strangely, the air in the tunnel smelled fresh and clean.

He came to a chamber and peered around the corner of a large rock, and came face to face with a snarling, oversized black feline. Zokar froze, then saw the hand holding back the large cat by the scruff of the neck.

The cat growled and a familiar voice said, 'Quiet, Gan.'

There was another moment of silence, then the owner of the hand stuck his face around from behind the cat. It was a long-haired, tanned and slightly thinner Shiva Kiran, whose blue eyes registered astonishment and delight.

'Zokar?' it was a whisper.

'Captain.'

Shiva Kiran smiled and sighed, 'Am I glad to see you.'

'Shall we go?'

'Where?'

'Back to the fleet. A shuttle left the ship at the same time as I jumped, the troops will be here shortly.'

'The fleet? You brought a fleet? Where did you come from?'

'Well, I didn't quite bring a fleet. I came back from the Core. There's a bit of a battle going on up above us, and we, the Terrans and I, have commandeered a few ships. It's a long story.'

Shiva stared at Zokar, taking it all in, 'The Terrans and you? You came back from the Core?'

'I was taken there as a prisoner, then when I was, er, released, I obtained a ship and came back for you.'

'Why?' Shiva asked.

The elf bowed his head, turned and started out of the cave without giving an answer.

Shiva stepped out the cave and walked over to Zokar. He stood beside the tall, sombre elf, waiting for the shuttle to descend. Zokar's eyes shifted across to him a couple of times, but he said nothing.

Then Zokar noticed the large catlike creature emerge from the cave, followed by another golden cat with blue eyes and asked, 'You have adopted predators?'

'They come in handy.'

Silence fell again.

Shiva said, 'I thought I was going to die here. Thanks for coming back for me.'

'They are a powerful and dangerous breed, these Terrans. I did not like your chances, not with the anarchy that would have prevailed after the Great Awakening.'

'Bit risky for you, coming back here, then.'

'Hmmm.'

Shiva gave up. Sometimes, he thought, you just have to accept that your friends are aliens. Shiva stroked Gan's ears soothingly, as Ghrian sniffed curiously at Zokar's ankles.

A thought struck Shiva, 'Did you find the Empress's daughter yet?'

'Yes. I managed to get her on board the Reingold, but then we were challenged by a Union fleet and I was taken prisoner.'

Shiva frowned, 'Why didn't you run when they challenged you? The Reingold is fast enough to get away from a Union ship. You had the Empress's daughter.'

'That was not an option. They were threatening to destroy this planet's surface.'

'So?'

Zokar glared at Shiva and said, 'You were down on the surface at the time.'

Shiva grinned and said, 'You old softy.'

'Insult me like that in front of the crew and I will blast you,' Zokar said irritably.

'I know,' Shiva smiled.

Shiva looked up, waiting for the shuttle to arrive. Zokar snuck a look over at him and was surprised to see the smile remain on his companion's battle hardened young face as Shiva surveyed the blue sky.

They watched as the shuttle descended steeply, then lifted slightly before planting itself in a small cloud of dust twenty metres in front of them. Several troops jumped out and fanned out, scanning the area, then stood to attention.

A slight, pale-headed figure stepped down out of the shuttle and walked towards them. Female, saw Shiva, then his mouth dropped open and so did hers as she looked up at him.

'You!'

'You're Shiva?' Laura said.

'You, from the electronics store,' Shiva said.

'The way you spoke, 'a communications device', huh, I should have known,'

Zokar was puzzled, 'Wait, you two know each other?'

'Not yet,' Shiva said.

'Not really,' Laura said at the same time and blushed, looking pleased, 'But somehow, I think that's going to change.'

'Shiva, this is Laura,' Zokar said and headed for the shuttle. Shiva and Laura followed more slowly.

The two huge cats followed Shiva and Laura looked at them askance, 'What are those?'

Shiva looked at her, and said, 'Those are my cats. I found them here.'

She stared at Gan and Ghrian oddly and Shiva asked, 'What is wrong?'

'Well, they're not... they're not Earth cats, Shiva. They're not Terran, I mean.'

Shiva turned in surprise to look at his two companions, 'They're not?'

'No. They're no species I recognise.'

'Huh, that's odd,' Shiva said, but headed for the shuttle with Gan and Ghrian. He caught up with Zokar.

'What, they're coming with us?' Zokar asked.

'Of course,' Shiva said.

Zokar raised his eyes to the blue sky above them and exchanged a look with Laura, who shrugged and followed Shiva and the two cats back to the shuttle. After a quick glance around, Zokar followed.

# CHAPTER THIRTY-FIVE

The united, fully operant minds of the inhabitants of Earth were all busy. They had a planet to defend. From the minds they had contacted amongst the occupants of the Union ships, they had gained sufficient military intelligence to know that the Union was a real and immediate threat to their planet's security.

The humans worked hard to create more mind-shields. Gold mines were ramped up to full production capacity and factories sprang up beside the mines to product the delicate-looking headpieces.

On the surface, shipyards sprang up and the humans started building spaceships, using the technological knowledge they had gained from the Union ships' crews.

They worked fast and every person could access any required knowledge, to perform any task, immediately and easily from the group mind. The logistics of this meant that at any time of the day or night, they could have hundreds of engineers, hundreds of plastics technicians, hundreds indeed of any type of expert they required. This made the shipbuilding effort swift, without sacrificing quality. Everyone knew how to do everything just right. It was an amazing way to work and surprisingly, the Terrans thrived on it. For such an independent, violent race, they suddenly seemed to change their very natures, just as the animals had done. The naturally violent, predatory nature of the Terran humans towards each other evaporated in the face of an outside threat to their planet.

Forty ships were built in two weeks. They did not have sufficient gold to build any more. Gold was used in hyperdrive cores, too, which was why it was in such demand.

At the end of the two weeks, the Earth ships floated up out into the atmosphere and Zokar Rizian saw them for the first time. He stared at them and turned to Shiva, standing beside him on the bridge of the Reingold, 'Is it just me, or are those ships,'

Shiva was staring at the view screen with the same wonder that showed on the faces of the rest of the control room crew.

'It's not just you, Zokar,' he whispered.

The reason for their amazement was that the Earth ships were beautiful. Instead of the hulking grey conglomerates of the Union Ships, or the plain black, scarred tubular form of the Reingold, the Earth ships were the same deep, opalescent blue of the planet below them and were streamlined with long, graceful curves.

Laura looked around, her jaw dropped and she said softly, 'Oh, they look like dolphins, only blue.'

'What is a dolphin?' Shiva asked and she looked askance at him.

'It is a marine mammal found on Earth,' she explained.

'The ships are moving. They're flexible. How did they access the technology to do that?' Zokar said, impressed by the ingenuity of the Terrans.

'I guess they had Earth's artists and all the marine biologists and all of the Union's know-how to build ships.' Laura paused, 'You know it's human nature to customise our rides,' she smiled.

'I don't understand why they are streamlined,' Trudi said, 'As they will be travelling in a vacuum. There's no water flow or airflow to slow them down?'

'A common misconception,' Shiva said, 'is that space-time behaves the same at rest as it does when a ship travels in hyperdrive.' He was still entranced by the beautiful ships before him, noticed Zokar.

Zokar took over the explanation from Shiva, 'It is an additional defence. Normally when a Union battle cruiser is travelling at full speed in hyperdrive, its shields provide the streamlining, as they surround the vessel much like a cowling on a land vessel. In case of catastrophic failure of the shields at full hyperdrive, the streamlined design of these new Terran vessels would give them some protection against the wormhole ripping them to pieces.'

'Or,' Shiva hesitated and said, 'I saw some Greys leaving Earth after the Terran group mind went operant.' He looked worried.

'So?' Zokar asked.

'The Greys are from Andromeda, correct?' Shiva asked.

'Correct,' Zokar said.

'So how did they get here?' Shiva asked.

'Presumably in very fast ships,' Zokar replied.

'But it would have taken them at least a millennium. The distance between stars is nothing compared to the distance between galaxies such as ours and the Andromeda galaxy,' Shiva mused.

'Sleeper ships?' Laura suggested.

'No,' Zokar said, remembering what the Greys had said to him when they arrived, 'They were born in Andromeda.'

'How long do Greys live?' Laura asked.

Nobody knew. Shiva suggested, 'I suppose it would be some millennia.'

'Why?' Laura asked.

'I don't know, I just guess that they would live that long. Everything else does,' Shiva replied.

She stared at him oddly, and contemplated the view screen silently.

Zokar said, 'What has this all got to do with the streamlining of the Terran ships?'

Shiva said, 'The Greys may have discovered an even faster form of propulsion than hyperdrive.'

Zokar looked thoughtful, 'And you are wondering if the Terran humans have accessed that technological knowledge, through a stray Grey or two left behind on Earth when the Terran population formed a group mind?'

'Yes,' Shiva said and waved an expressive arm at the new Terran ships.

'Ahhh,' Zokar said.

'So wait,' Trudi asked, 'You're saying that this streamlining might not just be for aesthetics or extra safety, it might be because the Terran ships are capable of using a much more advanced propulsion system?' she looked disappointed.

'Exactly,' Shiva replied.

'Damn,' Zokar said.

'You know what?' Shiva mused.

'What?' Laura asked.

'I think I'm glad you're on our side,' he replied.

'How do you know what side I am on?' She looked directly at Shiva, her clear grey eyes betraying nothing, 'I have not said.'

Shiva looked at her, then at Zokar, then back at her, 'Actions speak louder than words,' Shiva said, then turned back to watching the beautiful forms of the Terran ships spread out.

The view screen burst into life and the now-young visage of General Mick McCosker appeared on it, with Nick, Karl, Ryan and the solemn Genevieve Harris at his side.

'Zokar,' he boomed, to Zokar's relief finally getting the pronunciation of his name right, 'How are you? Is this your friend Shiva?'

'We found our captain, yes, thank you,' Zokar said coolly.

Shiva raised an eyebrow but said nothing.

The general smiled, then spotted Laura, 'Hey, who are you?'

'Laura St James,' Laura answered.

'Hi. Do you work for those two?'

'You might say that,' she smiled. Shiva and Zokar stepped up to flank her.

'Well, stick with them, love, they'll look after you,' grinned McCosker, gaining him a raised eyebrow from Laura. She shook her head but said nothing.

'General, we have pressing ship's business. Is it alright if I contact you in a few minutes?' Zokar asked.

'Yes, of course.'

When he had gone, Zokar asked Laura, 'Is it just me, or did the General just comment a cultural misdemeanour? I would not hold it against him, Laura, for he has been instrumental in saving your planet.'

Laura looked at Zokar, 'One day, Zokar, you're going to realise just how afraid of me you should be.'

Zokar gave a small, ironic bow, smiling, 'When that day comes, my lady, I will depart your presence. Not for fear, but because it is at that point where I will have outlived my usefulness to you.'

Shiva chuckled, because he could not imagine Zokar doing anything through fear.

She looked at Zokar, then smiled at Shiva, 'A real shithead, isn't he?'

'That is why I like him,' Shiva smiled.

'Yeah, me too,' Laura smiled and patted them both on the shoulder as she walked towards the control room exit.

'My lady, may I ask where you will be?' Zokar asked.

She stopped and smiled at them, 'Shiva, if you would kindly assign me some quarters, I will try to sleep. Earth is well protected,' she waved an arm at the blue ships now heading out to the edge of the Solar system, 'And in case you aliens haven't noticed, I haven't slept for about 36 hours.'

'Use my quarters,' Shiva offered, 'I will share with Zokar until a suitable arrangement can be made. This level, cabin one.'

'Thank you, kind sirs,' Laura smiled tiredly and left.

'Did I offer-'

'Shut up, Zokar,' Shiva smiled.

'Sir, look!' cried the helmsman.

A ghostly white light was now enveloping Earth and floated about it like a soft, fluctuating halo.

'Scans! Some sort of attack?' Zokar said.

'No sir, there are shuttles travelling within it.' The helmsman replied.

Zokar was gazing intently at his view screen, 'Damn, they are quick learners.'

'What is it?' Shiva asked, relaxing a little.

'It appears to be a shield, a protective inertia field around the Earth. It restricts anything from moving any faster than the speed of sound in Earth's atmosphere. It is... an inertial damper.'

'A shield? They built their own suppression field?'

'Yes, but not like the original suppression generator, this is simply a damper to physical movement. It will protect them from fast-moving ships or weapons. Some sort of stasis technology. Very, very clever. And the temporal depression it makes is what is causing the white halo effect.'

'Holy smokes, these people learn fast,' Shiva muttered and Zokar nodded his agreement.

Zokar came over to stand beside Shiva, and said quietly enough so that only Shiva could hear him, 'What do you think annoyed her about the General, Shiva?'

'You didn't get that?'

'No, I am sorry. She is more human than elvish in her thinking.'

'Which you should be used to, dealing with me all the time,' Shiva smiled, but went on to explain, 'I think she was annoyed that the General asked her where *her* allegiance lay. She's the Empress's daughter, for the galaxy's sake, Zokar. He should have been asking us whether *our* allegiance was to her.'

'But does he know that she is the Empress's daughter? Perhaps it was a simple mistake.' Zokar said.

'True, but I think she was rather peeved at being called 'love,' too. The general has a lot to learn about women,' Shiva added with a chuckle.

'Ah, I see.'

'I would guess it might be a touchy subject. A female like her, with intelligence and abilities, raised by savages who are by turns violent, demeaning, and condescending towards their females. I would suggest it is a minefield we ourselves want to avoid, Zokar.'

'So you don't trust her? I thought you liked her?'

Shiva smiled and sighed, 'I guess you don't understand the phrase 'hot and dangerous?'

Zokar raised his eyebrows, then turned to admire the receding view of the blue Terran ships as they departed.

'I wonder where they're going?'

# CHAPTER THIRTY-SIX

That evening Shiva left the bridge with Gan and Ghrian flanking him and walked to his quarters. He remembered the last minute that they were occupied and headed instead for Zokar's door. It swished open, which was unusual, as Zokar was very security conscious. Shiva grinned when he heard it click and lock several times behind him and the big cats. Ah, Zokar, true to form.

'Where are you, Zokar?'

'Here,' came a muffled response and Shiva wandered into Zokar's sleeping quarters. The two big cats settled down inside the doorway, sleepy after a long day on the bridge.

The elf was gazing at his computer screen, which showed a black-haired elf screwing his face up in concentration and asking, puzzled, 'My father says you came back for me, why would you do this?'

'Hey. What are you watching?'

'Shhhhh! It's really good.'

Shiva shook his head. Terran culture was insidious. The Terrans seemed to have wonderful imaginations and invented story after story, which they then went to great trouble to act out and then publish in audio-visual format. They called them 'movies.' His crew had one by one fallen victim to the lure of these soap operas, but Zokar? Zokar was the last one Shiva had expected to become enamoured of any such thing.

'They have elves on those movies?'

'He's not an elf. Shush.'

'Oh, I do beg your pardon,' chuckled Shiva, taking off his boots. He stretched out on Zokar's bed, next to the elf who was sitting watching the movie intently, 'What's the difference?' he added.

Zokar shot him a glare, 'They have green blood and come from a desert planet. They are totally different from elves.'

Shiva smiled. He remembered as a child, visiting the planet of the elves. It was like a paradise, with steep mountains, lush greenery, silver oceans. It had been a shock for Shiva and his mother to learn that the planet had been almost destroyed only weeks after they had left. With the destruction of its moon, half the planet's surface, the half that was facing the moon, was rendered uninhabitable, including the city where, Shiva had since learned, Zokar had grown up.

He stared up at Zokar's face, wondering how much of the hardness of the elf was due to that loss. How many friends did he lose, wondered Shiva. Was Zokar's murderous nature and cold, brutal attitude because of the destruction of his home? Had the elf once been a gentle creature like the one Shiva saw now on the computer screen, gazing curiously at his human companion?

Shiva pursed his lips and thought, no, I can't see it. Zokar has always been cold, and always will be, he thought.

'Laura likes you,' Zokar's voice surprised Shiva.

'She does?'

'Yes. The way she looks at you, it is obvious even to an elf like me. Also, her pheromone levels spike every time you walk within two metres of her.'

Shiva grinned, then asked, 'What do you think of her, Zokar?'

'I think she is wise.'

'Why? I mean, what in particular makes you think that?'

'She is protecting her home planet. That is wise. A creature without a home is forever damaged, never whole.'

Had Zokar read his mind? Did he know what Shiva was thinking? Shiva saw the hollow look in Zokar's eyes and put his hand on Zokar's shoulder and said, 'I'm sorry, my friend. Sometimes we all forget.'

Zokar looked down at the human and nodded, pursing his lips, 'Laura understands what is at stake here. Many would not realise, until it is too late.'

Shiva nodded and tightened his lips. He looked at Zokar and asked, 'Are you alright, Zokar?'

'I am now.'

Shiva nodded, 'By the way, thanks.'

'For rescuing you?'

'Yes.'

'You are welcome,' the big elf shrugged. Shiva nodded off to sleep, but several hours later woke up hungry. He was still catching up from being half-starved on Earth for so many weeks. Zokar had propped himself back on the pillows and was watching more movies, violent ones from what Shiva glimpsed on the screen.

Shiva sat up sleepily and squeezed Zokar's shoulder, 'Come, my old friend, let's eat.'

They stood up and Shiva led the way out of the cabin. The two big cats stood, looked at each other, then shadowed them on huge silent paws. Some of the crew who normally wouldn't see the captain and second officer, except if they visited the bridge, were startled by the two huge felines behind their senior officers.

Zokar felt a strange warmth in the palm of his hand and found to his surprise that the golden cat, Ghrian, had nuzzled him gently as it followed down the corridor. Zokar let his hand drift up and give the big cat a gentle stroke on the head, then pulled his hand away.

He pondered Shiva's attraction to Laura. They would mate, it was inevitable. There would be offspring. So long as Shiva did not, on his deathbed, put a geis on Zokar, to care for his descendants. Zokar took in a hissing breath. He would be forced to live whilst Shiva had living descendants. The elf sighed. Maybe if he kept silent, it would not happen. He sincerely hoped that it would not happen. Zokar could not see himself as a babysitter.

When they walked into the crowded mess, Zokar noticed Laura eating, with her mysterious dark-haired sister. Laura's eyes lit up like stars when she saw Shiva and Shiva shot a happy glance at Zokar before greeting her. Oh, yes, thought Zokar, there will be offspring. He smiled to himself and started to plan strategies for avoiding babysitting.

Zokar noticed that his cousin Elesk was also in the mess, sitting next to Trudi and wondered why she choked on her food when he smiled at her and Trudi. He shook his head, puzzled, but then his eyes drifted back to Trudi, and stayed there. Elesk had told him the story of how Trudi had rammed the Union battle cruisers with the Reingold and Zokar was in awe of the fiery dark-haired beauty. Trudi glanced in his direction and Zokar felt oddly disconcerted by her gaze.

The two big cats, Gan and Ghrian, wandered over and presented themselves politely at the kitchen door. They waited for the two large stainless steel buckets full of red meat to come out, then ate quietly. Normally they both went and wormed under the table at Shiva's feet, but Ghrian, the golden one, looked under the table and decided instead to settle behind Zokar's chair. He put his big golden head on his paws and gazed at the elf.

When the humans and elves rose after dinner, Ghrian sat up then fell into place behind Zokar, as if he had always been there. Shiva noticed, but said nothing, just gave a slight smile, and the black cat Gan, moved closer to fill the space behind Shiva that had been left by Ghrian's unexpected absence.

When they arrived back at the cabin, they sat to talk, and Zokar noticed the golden cat put a paw on his foot before falling asleep curled up in a purring ball at his feet.

Shiva smiled, 'I think you have been adopted, my friend.'

'He could choose a more sympathetic master,' Zokar commented drily, as he reached down and gently rubbed the base of the big cat's pointed ears. Ghrian purred loudly.

The other cat, Gan, lay at Shiva's feet quietly, but his eyes went from Ghrian, to Zokar, up to Shiva's face, and back again. Then he put his head down, but did not sleep, simply watched as the two men talked long into the night.

The next morning, on the bridge, the golden cat Ghrian, instead of following Shiva and Gan to the centre of the bridge, walked silently behind Zokar Rizian over to his station, then curled up at Zokar's feet. The bridge crew walked carefully around him, so as not to step on his tail. No-one said a word to Zokar about his new shadow.

The only time Ghrian rose was when Zokar wandered for no apparent reason over to Shiva's chair. Ghrian sat up and watched the elf's every step and curled up to sleep again when Zokar returned to his own console chair.

That evening at dinner, Gan stared, disappointed, at the dead food in his bucket. He sighed and started to eat, then looked at the food replicator. He left his meal and trotted off to find a handy human. Shiva was unavailable, having decided to catch up with some long-needed sleep in Zokar's cabin.

An hour later, the young ensign grumbled, 'I don't know what I'm doing here. And what does it mean, 'non-terminated protein food options'?'

Gan put an impatient paw up to the computer and the ensign kept typing, 'Oh alright, there, I've reprogrammed the food replicators for you. As soon as it detects that big paw of yours, or your littermate's, the replicator will automatically revert to these protein food options you've had me program into it. Happy?'

Gan purred loudly, stood up and trotted out.

The ensign glared after the big cat, and got back to his usual work, the much more important galley stocks review which he had been working on before Gan's unexpected arrival. His supervisor arrived about two minutes later, and asked, 'What have you been doing? You should have been finished this an hour ago.'

'Oh, I was helping the captain's cat. He wanted some additional menu options programmed into the food replicators.'

'Are you mad? The captain's cat is an Earth panther. It can't communicate with you. Consider yourself on report.'

The ensign glared angrily after his supervisor as she left and muttered, 'Earth panther my ass.'

Gan was hungry, but he debated tracking down Shiva first. He was uncomfortable when he was too long away from Shiva's side. He lifted his head and sniffed. Shiva had passed by here one point six minutes ago, in the direction of the mess hall. Gan bounded back towards the mess hall, then slowed to a dignified walk as he entered.

Shiva stared at the remains of Gan's previous meal, a silver bucket still piled high with raw fish and beef chunks, sitting outside the entrance to the kitchen. Shiva shivered and walked to his usual table and sat down with Zokar and Laura. The cat, Ghrian, was no-where to be seen and Gan had walked past his food and their table which concerned him.

'How are you going, Zokar, Laura?' Shiva said.

'Captain, I was just telling Laura here that I was wondering who was reprogramming the food replicators. The programming seemed to be coming from the galley computer. Do we have some special diets coming on line?'

'I don't think so,' but Shiva was distracted, because Gan had *crouched* in front of the replicator. Crouched like he was about to pounce on something? And was he wriggling his tail end back and forth?

'Gan,' Shiva started to say, worried, but he stopped because there were about a dozen shrieks from around the replicator and something was pouring out of the replicator opening in the wall and running out.

Several somethings, about the size of cats, but looking like alien rodents with six legs and furry bodies. Several crewmembers, male and female, jumped up onto tables.

Gan leapt into action. Within six short leaps, rolls and a gallop across the mess hall, with a final snap of his huge teeth, he had acquired all of the oversized rodent-like alien creatures. He crouched, tail swishing and almost knocking over three crewmembers while crunching on his writhing, squealing catch. He pinned them with his paws and ripped off their heads one by one. Eventually the creatures were still and the mess hall was dead quiet. All eyes were on Gan. Green blood from the alien rodents streaked the floor. One yeoman started sobbing.

Gan sat up, licked his paws, then looked around and picked up a mouthful of the now-dead rat-creatures and trotted over to Shiva's table, a group of furry, freshly killed corpses bobbing up and down from his jaws. He dumped them on the table next to Shiva and went back for two more. The largest one, he saved for last. He walked up to Shiva and respectfully deposited it at the Captain's feet on the floor, then nudged it with a paw towards Shiva. Then he sat next to Shiva and started crunching through his dinner.

'Ahhhh!' Zokar exclaimed happily, 'Now I know what that part of the programming meant.'

Shiva turned numbly to look at Zokar and Laura started giggling.

'What part?' Shiva asked.

'I think,' Laura giggled, 'He means the 'non-terminated protein food options'.'

Gan crunched through a particularly bony part of his dinner and Shiva put his head in both hands and groaned, 'Get a cleaning crew in here. And Gan…'

The big black feline looked up at him blissfully unaware that his actions could have upset the humans around him. 'Gan, from now on, if you want to eat your 'non-terminated protein food options', how about we set up a food replicator on the hangar deck, so you can chase them around to your heart's content?'

Gan purred loudly and nudged his head briefly against Shiva's shoulder.

Shiva smiled, but glanced up and caught the look in Zokar's eyes. The elf was looking distracted and Shiva knew why. They might as well relax while they could, because these few days might be their last.

The Opal ships had reported that morning that the full Galactic Union fleet had been mobilised. A thousand battle cruisers were now on their way at full hyperdrive towards Earth.

# CHAPTER THIRTY-SEVEN

Laura was talking intently to one of the Terran Generals on the communications link, Shiva noticed as he waited at the cabin door. He recognised him as the one that Zokar had called McCosker several times.

'They must not be in hyperdrive when it happens General, do you understand? The Opal ships, our blue ships, can take it, but the Union Battle Cruisers that we have commandeered will be destroyed.'

Shiva's ears pricked up and he stared at Laura.

'But if we're baiting them and we're running away, if we drop out of hyperdrive, they'll shoot us,' objected McCosker's voice from the communications link.

'That's right. I don't want our forces in the Union Battle Cruisers to have anything to do with baiting the Union forces. The Opal ships will have to harass the Union into responding. However, I want the Union to be under no doubt who they're dealing with, so for a few days before we start the deployment manoeuvres, the blue ships will need to skirmish alongside the existing Terran forces, okay?'

'Yes ma'am,' the General said.

'I want the Opal ships to move naturally to the fore and the other ships to drop back. We'll make it look like the Opal ships are protecting the older ships. Then we'll let the Opal ships get little too far out in front so the Union Battle Cruisers will go into hyperdrive to attack them and we'll deploy. But there must be an agreed signal, none of our non-Opal ships must be in hyperdrive when this weapon is deployed.' Laura paced the cabin.

'Absolutely, Ma'am.'

'Any questions?' she asked.

'Ma'am, what is the range of this weapon?' McCosker asked.

She was silent for a moment, 'We estimate fifty thousand light-years.'

Shiva went white and stepped forward into the room, 'Laura?'

She hushed him with a hand, 'General?'

McCosker's voice had gone quiet, 'Ma'am, that's half the Galaxy.'

'And?' Laura said.

'Ma'am, I feel constrained to point out that with a range that vast, the effect will extend far beyond the front lines of the Union. It will encompass half the Union itself. There may, no, there will, be civilian ships within that range. Unless they are warned,'

Shiva thought to himself, McCosker has been doing his homework.

Laura said, 'Understood, General. However, unless we wish to warn the Union forces, no warning can be issued.'

McCosker looked grim, but nodded.

'General, if you have a better idea for protecting Earth, now is the time to express it,' she said.

He was silent.

'Very well,' she said, 'You have your orders. If you need any more direction, contact me.' She cut the communications link and turned to Shiva.

'What is it, Shiva?'

He stared at her, wondering at the mentality that could coldly authorise such a thing.

'Could you at least let me warn my people? The Galactic Traders?' he asked, quietly.

She thought for a moment, 'The warning cannot be specific. We can't risk the Union getting wind of this. Your people may ignore it.'

'It's their only chance.' Shiva said

'Very well, get Zokar in here and we'll try to figure out a way to minimise casualties, both civilian and Traders. You have two days.'

'Thanks, Laura.'

But Shiva was shaking his head in disbelief still when he found Zokar in his cabin, with the golden cat Ghrian sleeping at his feet. These Terrans, thought Shiva, maybe I should be afraid of them, especially of Laura.

'Zokar, we have a problem,' Shiva said.

The elf looked up in silent enquiry.

'Do you know about the new weapon that the Terrans have developed?' Shiva asked.

'Not specifically. What sort of weapon is it?'

'It destroys everything moving faster than light speed with a radius of fifty thousand light years.'

Zokar raised his eyebrows. Zokar was elvish. Shiva sometimes came hard up against elvish indifference, and it chilled him to the bone. But this was different. Shiva was sure that even his elvish friend would react to this. To kill every living thing moving at speeds in excess of the speed of light, over the breadth of half of their own galaxy was unconscionable.

Zokar shook his head and looked up at Shiva, his eyes unreadable, and said, 'Ingenious.'

Shiva stared at Zokar, and felt ice wash through his soul for the second time in ten minutes. He thought of Laura and her coldness and he looked at Zokar in this moment and saw the same chilling coldness. That's right, she's part elvish, too, Shiva remembered. Perhaps it is the elvish part of her that is this cold, as it is in Zokar.

'I need-,' Shiva sprinted to the bathroom of Zokar's cabin and hurled up his dinner.

'Shiva?' Zokar said in alarm, 'You are not well!'

Zokar brushed him away and said, 'Don't touch me. Don't even look at me!'

Zokar backed away, confused and asked, 'Is it contagious?'

Shiva, his hands closed white-knuckled over the rim of the sonic toilet, whispered something.

'What did you say?' Zokar asked.

'I said,' Shiva rasped out, 'That I can only hope so.' He wiped his chin and stood back up, stepped over to the basin, rinsed out his mouth, then gathered his wits and walked out to face Zokar, 'Come on, we have to figure out a way to save as many lives as we can.'

He strode out of the cabin and although Zokar followed him and caught up with the swiftness that was native to his people, Shiva still felt more alone in that moment than he had ever felt in his entire life.

He walked into Laura's cabin, and stopped, then declared, '*Compassion.*'

'Shiva?' Laura asked, looking up from where she sat before the communications unit. She did not seem surprised by his abrupt entrance, but appeared a little puzzled by his comment.

'Compassion, that-' he looked around to encompass Zokar in his accusation, '-is what you both lack. You,' he turned back to face Laura, '-have just described a weapon and an attack plan which would wipe out a significant percentage of half the galaxy's population,' he glared at her, then turned his glare to Zokar, 'and your response when I described this to you? You commented on the 'ingenuity' of the weapon with no consideration of its devastating effect on innocent lives.'

'Shiva,' Laura said softly, 'I'm not happy about this. But you don't understand, it is imperative that I protect Earth.' She rose to her feet.

'At what cost?' cried Shiva his voice rising, 'At what cost? Is that insignificant little planet of yours so important that you would wipe out a sizeable chunk of humanity just to protect it?'

'Hey, we didn't start this war. The Galactic Union has used our home as a prison for thousands of years, remember?'

'I can't imagine why the Galactic Union thinks that Terrans should be locked up, if this is the Terran idea of galactic justice!' he was almost yelling, but still managed to instill his words distinctly with sarcasm.

She raised her voice and stepped towards him in response, 'Are you forgetting that they then threatened to blow us up?'

'I'd blow you up too if you weren't on my ship!'

'What sort of illogical-' Laura stopped yelling as Zokar stepped between them and put a hand on Shiva's shoulder.

'Shiva, perhaps-' Zokar started.

Shiva brushed his hand away, 'You're just as cold as she is! You called it 'ingenious'!'

Zokar spoke firmly, 'If you have any ideas as to reducing the range of the effect of this weapon, or otherwise controlling its impact  now would be a good time,' he looked at them both, 'either of you?'

They both said nothing and glared at each other, and eventually Zokar said, 'After all, isn't that why we are here?'

Laura took a deep shuddering breath and finally tore her eyes from Shiva's, 'Yes, yes, Zokar, you are right. Shiva, sit down!'

He was stunned. He was captain of this vessel, and nobody told him what to do. He started to protest, but Zokar put up a hand and stopped him, 'Shiva, please '

Shiva glared at Laura, 'Alright,' he grumbled and sat down.

'So, is there any way we can reduce its range?' Zokar asked.

It would be impractical, they decided, to try to warn the civilian population because the Union fleet might discover the nature of the new weapon and many civilians would simply ignore any warning to drop out of hyperdrive unless it came from the Galactic Union itself. Therefore the Terrans would send two Opal ships around the flank of the Union fleet and try to ascertain the range over which the Union ships were dispersed. Once those two ships reported back to the Terran forces, the weapon's power would be reduced to cover the space encompassing the main body of the Empirical forces.

Shiva sighed and rubbed his eyes. It was late. 'Well, that's decided, then?'

'Yes,' Laura said.

'Good. Well, if you don't mind, Laura, I'm going to catch some sleep,' Shiva said.

'Of course. Oh, and Shiva?'

He stopped at her door.

'I'm sorry I yelled at you. And thank you for your input.'

He sighed and nodded, then turned to Zokar.

'I'll see you in five minutes,' Zokar said quietly.

Shiva hesitated, then nodded and left.

Laura raised her eyebrows at the tall, imposing elf, 'You have something to say which you do not wish Shiva to hear?'

Zokar nodded, 'A few things.'

'Fire away,' she said tiredly.

'Shiva's mind is not mathematical, Laura. He does not see numbers like you or I do.'

'You mean the six billion lives on Earth?' she challenged him.

'Versus the one hundred and twenty thousand in the fleet. I see the logic in your position. I am not sure that he does. He is human.'

'Do you think Shiva will try to stop me from deploying the weapon?'

Zokar looked thoughtful, then shook his head, 'No. He will do as he says he will. And I trust that you will do the same.'

'I have no need to do otherwise, Zokar. If I find myself at odds with someone, I can ignore them.'

'Yes. That is the other thing that I wish to discuss with you.'

'Oh?'

'Shiva is attracted to you.'

'You think so? Maybe after tonight he has changed his mind.'

Zokar thought about that, 'He would not be put off by a perception of coldness in your nature. He has been my friend for seven years now and he tells me I am cold.'

'What's your point?'

'I do not believe his attraction to you is wise.'

She stared at him for a long moment, 'What makes you say that?'

'The level of power which you have achieved until now, is nothing, I believe, to what you will achieve in the near future.' Zokar said.

'You think I would hurt him?'

'If the attraction were to develop to more than just that, and you became lovers, is there not a chance that he may at some stage irritate you?'

'Well, I think we've just seen a pretty good indication that that can happen, yes.'

'And you are not worried that you may slip and use your powers against him?'

'You are concerned for his welfare?'

'Of course.'

She sighed, steepled her fingers and looked thoughtful for a while. Then she looked up at him, silver eyes meeting silver, 'I will not harm Shiva, I can tell you that. But Zokar,'

He looked into those unfathomable eyes, as she continued, 'Are you sure you want to relinquish him to me?'

'He is not mine to relinquish,' Zokar said.

She laughed and said, 'Oh, so you do have a sense of humour.'

He stared at her, then said, 'He is my friend, and my conscience. That is all.'

Laura said quietly, 'I'll give it some thought and get back to you, okay?'

'Thank you.' He turned and left.

Laura sat for an hour, thinking about the two men. Perhaps like Zokar, she too, needed someone to be her conscience.

# CHAPTER THIRTY-EIGHT

Two days later the two Opal ships cloaked and went far back behind the Terran lines, then split and came back around, crossing enemy lines. They were gone a nerve-wracking three hours and could not risk transmitting any signals in case they were discovered behind enemy lines and shot down.

The control room of the Reingold was like a tigers' convention, with Laura, Shiva and Zokar vying for room to pace up and down in the restricted area. Gan and Ghrian had the common sense to hide under Shiva's and Zokar's chairs.

Then a faint signal came back from behind them and the two ships were confirmed safe. Shiva, Zokar and Laura breathed sighs of relief and a further message came through.

'Range of Union ships, six light years Corewards from here, to thirty light years. They're pretty tightly bunched, about twenty-four light-years apart at most,' Shiva said.

'Twenty-four light years. That may change as they chase our ships back,' Laura added.

'But we have no way of knowing how much they will spread out,' Shiva said.

'They won't go too far away from each other. They're in battle formation now,' Zokar said, inspecting the messages coming through his scanners. He turned to Laura, 'I'd say they will not spread out by more than about fifty light-years altogether when in skirmishes, they will suspect a trap and keep their ranks close.'

'Shiva, do you concur?' Laura asked.

'Yes, that makes sense,' Shiva agreed.

'I sure hope you two know more about Union fighting tactics than we do,' Laura said, then stepped up to the communications unit on Shiva's central chair and hit the button, 'General, are your teams ready? Do you have the range estimates and coordinates?'

'Yes, Ma'am.'

'Very well, implement Plan A,' Laura commanded, and strolled back to sit down in a spare seat near Zokar.

The graceful blue ships began to move out towards the Union lines, and there was an immediate increase in chatter on the communications links and the Union fleet started to swing into a tighter formation, anticipating an attack.

The two Opal ships broke away and darted off in different directions, and started to harass the Union fleet's flanks with sporadic fire. Bright blossoms of explosions against shields flowered. Then the Opal ships swung back and headed back towards the home fleet and Earth, slipping into hyperdrive. The Union fleet accelerated as one into hyperdrive, intent on pursuit.

Laura hit the communications button and there was a moment's hesitation in her voice, 'Activate Peregrine device.'

Zokar Rizian stood, admiring Laura. Shiva had chosen well, his love was a warrior, through and through and knew the meaning of protecting her home. Zokar glanced at Trudi, standing determined next to Laura. The dark-haired beauty was so human, so readable, and so different from Laura. Yet she, too, stood steadily and watched as Laura deployed the weapon that would protect their home planet.

On the Galactic Union ship at the head of the formation pursuing the Opal ships, the navigator frowned and leaned forward, 'Sir, there is a temporal displacement wave, of immense power, heading directly towards us from the direction of the Terran fleet. Impact in seventeen seconds.'

'We're in hyperdrive, lieutenant. It will have no effect.'

'Sir, there is an unusual quality to these readings. I think you should have a look,'

The General stood up and leaned forward to peer into the proffered computer screen, then a frown appeared on his face, 'That's... that's got a spatial component. It's an odd pattern. It seems to have an unusual sort of resilience, almost like it's self-repairing.'

'Could it be some kind of weapon?'

'No, it's a wave. It's not discriminate enough to be a weapon.'

'Some sort of side effect of something the Terrans have done?'

'No, I don't think so. Divert more power to shields. Bring them to maximum, just in case it breaches the hyperdrive barrier.'

'Aye, aye, sir,' the weapons officer said and they fell silent as the wave of displacement, invisible to the naked eye but apparent on their screens, came upon them rapidly.

The wave not only breached the hyperdrive barrier, but disabled their shields. Without shields, travelling at hyperdrive, the huge ship was torn apart from the outside, every projection glowing instantly white then vaporising in the force of the wormhole. The ship exploded into silent oblivion. Behind them, the other ships did the same.

Dom had been in the third ship with the Union fleet, still agonising over his decision to side with the Galactic Union against Laura and Earth. His mind had for twenty-two years been devoted to the mission of finding and restoring his sister to her rightful place in the Union and it was a shock to him to find out that she had other plans. It was even more of a shock to realise that she owed him nothing and having had no knowledge of his great quest, gave it little regard.

Nothing had turned out the way he had imagined it. She had not fallen into his arms and been delighted to find him. She had defended a home which was not hers, but had a strange, alien hold over her heart and soul. She had defied him, argued with him, and rejected him and the Galactic Union.

Dom had let his anger get the better of him, and had hit the hyperdrive button on his console with much more force than usual. The button jammed down and he stared down at it. .

'Sir,' his navigator said, horrified, watching the jammed down hyperdrive button and the readings which were flooding into his monitor with incredible speed. Something had gone terribly wrong....

Back on the Reingold, Laura stared blankly out at the space where the Union fleet had been. The fleet had simply blinked out. It seemed too clinical, too simple. But then she felt the faint link that she had shared with Dom, the link that was so much a part of her that she had never realised that it existed, fade out and go silent. She closed her eyes in shock and her knees sagged.

Dom, who had searched for her for twenty-two years. Dom, with whom she had argued horribly, who had wanted her to abandon Earth and go back with him to unite the Galaxy. Perhaps he had been right, maybe that would have been better for Earth than this. But still, she would have liked to get to know him.

Laura glanced across at Trudi and remembered that if things had been slightly different, she and Trudi would still be on Earth and would have been destroyed along with the planet. Trudi did not deserve to die. She had committed no crime, nor had many of the other humans on Earth. But the Union would have destroyed them all without recourse, without trial.

Several hours later, Laura stared blankly at the stars on the view screen. The last echoes of her mother's screaming voice had faded. Laura had tuned out half-way through, after Arlene had savagely declared war on Earth and swore she would hunt Laura down until her dying breath.

Zokar, in a rare display of anger, had hit the communications unit button so hard to silence it, that the unit had been smashed. He had looked at his fist in amazement, as if until that moment he had not known his own strength. Shiva stared with wonder at Zokar. For a being without a conscience, the elf was acting very strangely.

Laura clenched her eyes shut, and when they opened Shiva saw what he never thought to see, tears slipping unfelt down her pale face. He put an arm around her and to his surprise, Zokar came up on the other side of her and put his arm around Laura from the other side. They stood holding her, looking out at the stars and thinking of the thousands of lives in the Galactic fleet which had ended.

'My God, Shiva, what have I done?' Laura managed to say, eventually.

'You did what you had to. You saved Earth,' Shiva said.

'At what cost? First this, then Dom, and now,' she looked at the empty space where the Galactic Fleet had been and her eyes drifted down to the crushed communications button, 'this is war. Up until now, it has been just a couple of battles, a dispute over a planet on the Rim that wanted its freedom. Now this is real, honest-to-God, vengeance-driven, war. You heard my mother, she won't rest now until Earth is destroyed and I'm dead. So we don't know if Earth will survive anyway. Can we stand against the whole Galaxy?'

Shiva looked over her head at Zokar and said, 'I guess we'll find out.'

Zokar's eyes flicked from Shiva to Laura and back again, and he tightened his grip.

Laura said, 'I don't even know if we're on the right side any more.'

Zokar said quietly, 'We are.'

The other two both looked at him, Shiva and Laura both surprised at the absolute conviction in his deep elvish voice.

Trudi said nothing, but inched a little closer to Zokar. To her surprise, she felt the elf's fingers entwine around hers and he gave her a quick, shy smile.

# CHAPTER THIRTY-NINE

Trudi was intrigued by the tall silver-haired elf with the pointy ears with silver eyes. She was most intrigued by that unexpected gesture on the bridge, when he had taken her hand and how just for a moment she had glimpsed the shyness behind the stone exterior.

She was sensible enough to ask Shiva what would interest Zokar and was surprised at the answer, 'Chess.'

'Chess?'

'Yes. He loves chess. If you offered him sex or chess, he would choose chess every time.'

Laura raised her eyebrows and looked at Shiva.

'So you think I should offer him a game of chess?' Trudi asked.

'Or sex,' Shiva said casually. He looked Trudi up and down appraisingly, 'I don't think he would reject you. I could be wrong, though, ow!'

Laura had cuffed him soundly over the ear.

Trudi wandered out, and meandered through the large vessel. She stopped off at her room and used the replicator produce a chess board, then walked towards the elf's room and knocked, chess board and pieces under her arm.

'Yes?' the voice was terse, annoyed.

'Trudi.'

'Come in.'

She stepped through the door and saw Zokar sitting in front of his computer. He looked up, his face impassive.

Trudi was struck by a wave of shyness, but she managed to look him in the eye, 'Shiva said that a good way to get to know you would be to offer you a game of chess.'

The elf turned to her and chuckled, 'Did he now? Tell me,' he looked her up and down, 'Did he suggest any alternatives?'

'No' her voice was firm.

'Oh. Well, chess it is then.' He waved at the chair opposite his computer and pushed the computer away on its arm, giving them a clear space to play. She set up the board and gave him white, but he smiled and took black. She made the first move.

Two hours later, Zokar Rizian realised that he had been played to checkmate, by a human female. That was impressive and humiliating. He stared at Trudi, darkly.

She smiled and asked, 'Rematch?'

He nodded curtly and reset the board.

'I don't suppose,' Trudi asked, 'You have anything here I could drink?'

Zokar wordlessly fetched her a glass of water and she smiled at his lack of courtesy. She supposed that someone used to being waited on hand and foot would not have learned much courtesy over the years and she reminded herself not to chide him.

After she won the third game, he leaned back in his chair and surveyed her, then asked without preamble, 'Will you be my mate?'

'Zokar,' she chuckled, 'That is so damned elvish of you. You are not a gracious race, you know that? There are ways to ask, which are not so, I don't know.'

'Mmmm. I notice that you protest my phrasing, but you have not said 'no'.'

'No, I have not said no,'

Zokar raised his eyebrows, then stood up and stepped over to Trudi, pulling her to her feet easily. He ran his fingers down the side of her face and observed, 'You are very beautiful, but so human.'

'That's not a bad thing,' she whispered, breathless. The elf seemed frighteningly powerful and she caught the alien scent of him, and wondered if this was a good idea. Then her face was caught in two large, gentle hands and he leaned down and kissed her with cool lips. Trudi felt a strange tingling in all her nerves and shuddered.

'You are frightened of me,' Zokar whispered, the silver eyes close to hers.

'No.'

He pulled her into his arms and stroked her hair, 'Do not be.'

In the mess later that evening, Laura noticed the glow in Trudi's eyes. She asked quietly, 'Zokar?'

Trudi nodded happily.

Laura grinned. She did not really see what Trudi saw in the big silver-haired, grim looking elf, but her sister was contented with him. Also, the next time Laura saw Zokar Rizian she was struck by the change in his demeanour, he seemed almost cheerful, which was saying a lot about the grimmest person Laura had ever met. Well, good luck to them, thought Laura. It was two weeks before Shiva noticed, to Laura's amusement.

One morning, he came into her quarters, and said, 'You'll never guess what I just saw?'

Laura smiled, 'Trudi and Zokar?'

'How the... oh,' Shiva said. He went on, though, to comment, 'Of all the people I know, he is the last I would expect to enter into a relationship with a woman.'

Laura turned her head and looked at Shiva, then squinted in puzzlement. 'Why?'

'He's always been so self-contained, like he doesn't need anybody. I've known him for seven years, and he's never even looked at a girl.'

She smiled softly at him, 'And yet he turned his back on a trillion-credit ransom and fought his way across half a galaxy to rescue you.'

Shiva shuffled his feet, 'That's different. He is my friend. I would have done the same for him.'

'Yes,' Laura said, 'You know, I do believe you would have. I'm glad he's with Trudi. I have a feeling those two will look after each other.'

'I hope so, for his sake.'

She stood up and stepped closer to Shiva, correcting him, 'And for hers. She is my sister.'

'Yes, sometimes I forget. She is so human.'

'Humans aren't that bad,' she murmured and then took another step closer and stood on tiptoes to kiss her particular human.

# EPILOGUE

Far out in the intergalactic void, beyond the reach of even the most sophisticated scanners of Earth or the Galactic Union, lay a small space station. Grey aliens walked around inside its titanium hull, performing their minimal duties. A small flotilla of Grey ships floated neatly around the station.

The depression in the space-time continuum around the Grey alien base was widespread. Even so, it barely caught the fast-moving Galactic Union vessel at its edges. The battle cruiser slowly began to turn, and over time spiralled in towards the centre of the depression.

After three circuits, it was caught by the long range scanners of the Greys. Their scanning technician looked at his readouts with some surprise. The vessel had been moving at maximum hyperdrive, but as it approached the base, was claimed by the inertia of the depression and began to slow down. After several more circuits it was travelling at a slower and slower rate. Eventually it drifted passively towards their base.

Several Grey ships moved out to investigate the hulk, for hulk it turned out to be, mostly devoid of life. The twelve hundred humans and elves aboard had all passed away from the stress of being exposed to maximum hyperdrive for too long. But there was one life form which had survived that was of much greater interest to the Greys than the other twelve hundred put together.

# About the Author

Sam Taylor is an Australian author who has written over 98 short stories and several novellas. Since writing Deadly Jewel, Sam has been busy collaborating with a select group of writers to produce 'Tales from the Perseus Arm,' an anthology of science fiction short stories available on www.amazon.com as a Kindle, print and eBook.

Sam has finished writing the sequel to Deadly Jewel and is currently busy editing both that, and Volume Two of 'Tales from the Perseus Arm.'